AMERICAN BY BLOOD

AMERICAN BY BLOOD

Andrew Huebner

TRANSWORLD PUBLISHERS LTD
61–63 Uxbridge Road, London W5 5SA
A division of The Random House Group Ltd

RANDOM HOUSE AUSTRALIA (PTY) LTD
20 Alfred Street, Milsons Point, NSW 2061, Australia

RANDOM HOUSE NEW ZEALAND LTD
18 Poland Road, Glenfield, Auckland, New Zealand

RANDOM HOUSE (PTY) LTD
Endulini, 5a Jubilee Road, Parktown 2193, South Africa

Published by Anchor, a division of Transworld Publishers

First published in Great Britain by Anchor, 2000

10 9 8 7 6 5 4 3 2 1

Copyright © 2000 by Andrew Huebner

The right of Andrew Huebner to be identified as the author of this work
has been asserted in accordance with the Copyright, Designs and Patents
Act 1988

A catalogue record for this book is available from the British Library

ISBN 1862 30089 5

Design by Carla Bolte

Printed in Great Britain by Mackays of Chatham plc, Chatham, Kent

TO MY FAMILY

Turn your eyes to the valley; there we shall find
The river of boiling blood in which are steeped
all who struck down their fellow men.

—Dante's *Inferno*

AMERICAN BY BLOOD

— 1 —

They rode up over a trail to a rise with the three scouts in the lead. As they passed through a patch of juniper trees, the sun turned hot and the very air around them, with the sawing legs of the hoppers and the twits of the birds, seemed to hum with heat. Before them was a valley now with dew burning light on the spots of dying, browned grass. Tall sprigs of Queen Anne's Lace caressed the horses' legs and speckled the soldiers' boots with their sex.

Coming over a rise they saw the white things on the hills. Bradley's horse snorted, hesitating, sniffing the air. He kicked it on ahead.

Hah, he called to it.

No one else spoke.

Not even Shit, what in the hell, or Goddamn.

Maybe it was the smell, or the flies, or the wild dogs. The dogs were everywhere, they darted under the legs of their horses. They yelped wildly at their horses and gnawed brazenly at their boots. The soldiers kicked at them and hollered. The dogs had blood on their yaps. Their eyes rolled back white in their heads.

There were so many flies. A fog of them attacked the Private called Gentle, his eyes, nose, in his mouth when he yelled and cursed, kicked his horse's flank and rode through it.

The smell was like a film that permeated their souls through the pores of their skin. They drew their hankies and bandannas from their saddlebags and tied them around their noses like bandits. Their necks pricked and their backs tingled. From the south a crow cawed, then another. The big, black birds flapped overhead, close enough to Gentle that he could hear their wings. He ducked as they passed. When he looked around, no one was watching.

The Lieutenant's lead point, Private August Huebner, was the first of them to spot the dead. As he rode alongside the river he saw a horse and looked that way.

Its labored breathing sounded raw and strange, head all swelled, an empty eye-hole, leaking pus. Bradley drew his pistol and shot it. His hand shook a bit, and he had to use the other to steady.

Keep your eyes open, he said.

Dried blood had flowed in a path into a pond-like place, had turned the land under them black. Their horses stepped lightly on it, like they were walking now on some new surface.

There was blood in the dirt in sticky dark pools around each of the fallen that gathered in rivulets, recedes and indents of the landscape. There seemed to be blood even in the sky and wind. The scouting party had the hankies over their noses for the smell. They closed their eyes. Some of them retched right off their horses. They could not guard or flush their hearts.

Huebner saw a patch of wildflowers, purple and white wisteria, speckled with blood, bits of bone and brain in a perfect burst of color from the crown of a man's scalped head. He swallowed and kneaded his horse past.

Hands, heads, torsos, feet and legs, eyeballs, fingers and cocks cut off and scattered about, stiffening into grotesque and obscure mockeries of life. Birds hovered overhead, squawking horribly. The bodies were bloodied, swollen and discolored from two days in searing sun, covered by pulsing masses of flies. Three crows raised their heads lazily, like black princes at a castle feast, when Huebner kicked at them. Gentle's bullets buzzed past his shoulder, exploding each of them into a cascade of feathers.

A Bible had been ripped apart, strewn to the wind. They saw odd pages, stuck to bloody scalp-shed faces, floating in the hot breeze. Bradley tried to gather them up, got a pile together then stopped and threw them up in the air. It seemed really important at first, then it wasn't anymore. The bodies were left for rot on an earth tired and scarred by the fury of their dying.

They separated, the five of them in the scout party. They got off their horses and led them by the bridle, petting their noses and whispering in their ears. A man with his face peeled off and hanging: lips, nose cartilage and one eyeball hanging by a strand from his naked jawbone. Ancient, unknown markings were carved in his naked, hairless chest.

They had to fight off the wild dogs. They were feeding, the nasty bastards. They'd laugh, this terrible ear-splitting screech. Gentle, raising his rifle, got off four rounds at them, hitting two before Bradley tapped his shoulder.

That'll be enough of that, soldier, he said.

Private August Huebner pulled a man's teeth open and pushed his tongue back between them, and lay the head on a mound of grass. He felt like he had to do something. Another had died in a crouch, his mouth wide open. The top of his head brown, dried blood. Huebner tried to close at least his eyes, gently stroking the lids shut. He couldn't straighten out the body. The limbs were stiff, blue and hard. From the soldier's tightened fist hung a silver chain broken off as if in a last fight for its possession, or a last prayer. The Private left him just like that.

The sun moved behind a bank of clouds, and for a few minutes the morning became as dark as dusk. The men took their nervous horses to a gathering of trees and tied them there. A soft breeze blew on Bradley's sweat-soaked neck and shoulders. His horse tittered and he rubbed its hot flank with cool dirt taken from under the shade of the trees. When he looked to the distant mountains, purple in the hard light, a thousand fragments of rock shimmered like glass in the brilliant sunlight.

It was noon, the hottest part of the day. Bradley thought they should get back, but the thought of leaving made his stomach tingle. Everyone would wonder where they were, if something had happened. Then he forgot. Thirty minutes later he thought of it again and called over Huebner.

Ride and get the others.

Sir?

Huebner looked dazed, his eyes far-off.

This ain't what we come for, sir.

The words came from Huebner all at once. From the quiet Private it took Bradley by surprise.

Told us one white man was worth twenty-five Indians out here. Going to be like hunting.

Huebner stopped talking as suddenly as he'd begun. He looked down at his own hands, at the blood on them. He couldn't look Bradley in the face.

Take Brackett and Taylor! Bradley shouted, but he didn't know why. I'll stay here with Gentle, he said. Tell the Colonel what we've found.

For a moment Huebner just stood there nodding. When he finally turned his head, Bradley could tell he'd been crying. Huebner started to speak, but Bradley cut him off.

It's all right, Bradley said. Just go.

When they left, the Indians had burned brown the grass. Huebner and the others rode past the dead, some alone, others in groups, all of them stark white except their hands and faces turned dark by the sun. The three riders' shadows played out long over the sagebrush, dusty earth and the grasshoppers that flitted about by the score with every step their horses took. Huebner rode ahead of the others. Alone for a few moments on the dusty plains, he let his horse guide him back.

They done told us to come out here with y'all and scout for the battle, to back up Custer, Taylor said. He spoke with anger in his voice, a man who'd been lied to.

He don't need no back up, Brackett said. He worked his lips like he wanted to spit, but his mouth was dry.

Huebner reported to Colonel Gibbon and his staff, who, unbelieving of the words from his mouth but not the truth read on his solemn and wild-eyed countenance, set out themselves ordering an escort of fifty volunteers. Word got around. By the end of the day they all came, a straggling, incredulous entourage that stretched across the five miles from camp to the battlefield, pilgrims called to witness the defeat and demise of one of their own beliefs.

At most there were a half-dozen spades and shovels, picks and axes in the company. The soil was dry and porous. Shallow graves for a few, but most they just covered with brush or dirt, left them to the wild dogs and wolves.

The living became something else, stepped out of the lives they'd known and into others. They would never look at anything close to them, their mothers and fathers, brothers, sisters or their lovers, their old ragged first toys, the same.

Their lives long they tried to find what they had lost on that hill. Later, drunk, around fires they talked about what they could not, something in all the barrooms and prayer houses of their collective destiny they could never express. Maybe they knew this, but they talked anyway. They wanted to maintain at least the appearance of sanity. They said things like:

Goddamn.

It was just a big, open-air slaughterhouse.

It was like riding straight on into hell.

2

A north wind whipped the air down in the Medicine Tail Draw, ran it back against the face of the mountain. Nothing to burn but dead grass, sagebrush, seedling scrub pine. None of it caught real good, the smoke made matters worse. Gibbon's men had marched fifty miles in the last three days to join forces with Custer and come to find this.

They could not escape the smell. Bled their noses dry, tickled their brains silly. They soaked their bandannas and hankies in cold river water, laid wet cloths over their faces. Sleep came fitfully. Hard ground, dusty cyclones, sticker bushes and dirt mites. They cursed their devils and slapped their own faces. Fat, blood-laden mosquitoes, biting gnats.

Private Billy Gentle couldn't kill enough of them, wondered which had been with the dead.

Flies only live twenty-four hours, he said to a comrade. This is all they gonna know.

The other soldier just nodded at the kid. Gentle didn't wait, went off by himself. He meant the massacre, all they'll know of human life, feeding on the dead and the near, buzzing through air heavy with panic, agony and bloodlust. The horseflies were insistent, nagging. Soldiers smacked at them, left sticky, arterial-red blood spots on their clothes and skin. The flies' incandescent wings reflected the light of the dying sun.

The soldiers worked, in teams of two and three, to drag the bodies out of the coulee up to the hills, hard, demoralizing work. All day, bone tired, spooked.

They tried singing to their ladies, to their gods, to their mamas.

As the last of the sun sank red over the rounded buttes, to the distant west a rainbow stretched into blue night, no trace of rain. Yapping dogs, satiated, emboldened, roamed the camp, restless, barking and skittish at any attempt by the soldiers to make friends.

A Gavilan from Chesapeake County in Maryland took a line of string, a spring of an abandoned gun, went fishing, pale moonlight on silver water. Threw in his line, trawled a fly that just skimmed the surface. This motion, the old feel in his arms and hands would be the closest to calm he would get for a while. He wondered if the fish could smell the dead too. He didn't have much luck. There wasn't any left.

The stars began twinkling on way up.

A man yelled out as if in a dream.

He'd had enough.

Gunshots in the middle of the night echoed off the rock face. Morning found one of them dead. When they turned him over his eyes fell open, had a mouthful of dirt. An Evans from Baltimore, a Private with straight out buckteeth, a hare-lip and an attempt at a handlebar mustache, just long string wisps of hair. It didn't look good, but no one said this to his face. Someone remembered the march, kept falling down, till his pants ripped, his knee bloodied, turned to scab then bloodied again. A three-year-old just learning to run.

He'd always got up, the fellow said. Least 'cept till now.

No one had any idea why, no one question'd what he'd done.

Jim Thorne, a Maine volunteer with a drifter's distant eyes and a soft heart, had talked to Evans, like others did to the spooked horses.

They're just flies, he said.

They've gotten under m'skin. I can feel em, Evans told him.

We're all suffering somehows, son.

Not like me, Mister.

He yelled like a scared boy, jerked up from sleep, wakened by dreams, his voice high and keening.

When Evans suddenly reached out and hugged him, Thorne tried hard not to recoil from the dirt-streaked, greasy boy.

Hey, hey, son, what cha trying to do? he asked him.

Thorne slapped him on the chin but could not deter or embarrass the boy. He didn't know where he was.

C'mon now, ahh it's gonna be all right.

Just git them offa me, Evans yelled.

C'mon, son. They's just flies.

Thorne felt embarrassed to have to talk to another man like this. When he turned away, Evans grabbed his gun, put it to his head and pulled the trigger. An old Colt Peacemaker his father had given to him when he told where he was going.

Gun put a hole side his head ya could walk through.

It happened just like that, someone said. Whut-int nothing old Thorne could do.

Others told the next day, when they found the boy and pieced him together.

Only Thorne was close enough to see and he said little. Suicide was a mortal sin. He hadn't been to church on it, but his mama had Sundays his whole life, that was good enough for him.

Good a time as any, I giss, he said.

For the rest and whole of his life Thorne never said another word about the boy from Baltimore who died in his arms. Walked off from the crowd when they gathered around to a couple of gray horses, one spotted on the forehead, stark and ghostly they stood, against the black ground with the sky coming on to morning dressed in pale blue just above the line of their backs. Thorne got out his curry comb, brushed them down. He liked the way it felt to be with them this time of day.

Private Billy Gentle watched from a bluff, crouched like an eagle about to jump off into the sky.

Evans, at one point, had looked over at him, searching for something to fix his eyes on in the chaos of his last moments, but the glance that way only seemed to make it worse, as if whatever Gentle was doing was increasing his disquiet. Now Gentle quickly jumped up, cut through the crowd's embarrassed milling around to carry the poor boy up the hill.

What you gone to do? somebody asked him.

There ain't but one thing to. Standing around talking ain't it. Y'all can gimme a hand if ya will.

Some men didn't take to someone so young talking to them like that.

Others knew Gentle, so they didn't care.

A few stepped up, helped to carry the Chesapeake Evans up the hill.

That boy's a little fast with his words, someone said when they'd gone.

Hell, he's an idjit, what he is.

Better watch hisself is all.

You ever seen him shoot? Boy's one helluva crack, quick-draw shot.

I ain't looking to cross him, not with no gun, but I'll punch him iffin I git the chance.

Gentle and the others dumped Evans into a big hole, wiped hands on their pants and went back to what they were doing.

Gentle was playing a game. Some of the bugs were so fat and slow with blood it was possible to strike a match and burn them out of the air. He liked the t-sss sound it made. It was a way to pass the time toward dawn. He didn't like to sleep, ever, when other men were still awake. He felt for the horses. All night they snorted, as if trying to physically rend the smell from their nostrils. The horses tittered like after a storm, put Gentle to mind of a tornado that hit his family homestead once. Barns tossed on end, whole houses swept off in the winds. He watched the barn pulling off the earth, take off all at once. Horses there held on to the earth, like they were doing it right through their feet. The cyclone passed. There they were, standing in the very place where the barn had been moments before. For days after, the horses were queer. He would not sleep at all tonight. He knew this.

He looked over sleeping ranks of men, like little clumps of uneasy dead, black on dark rolling lush, night-blued hillside. Turning over, cursing, scratching, clawing at themselves like dogs.

They dug on in shifts during the night. No one liked the detail, but no one complained. They didn't want to leave them there, and no one wanted to stay even a minute longer than they had to.

As the night went on, more and more grabbed up their bedrolls and went down to the riverside. They washed their hands and soaked their heads. The smell followed them there. It had been with them the whole of the day and haunted them through the night, got into their clothes, mingled with the rank sweat of exhaustion and fear, the linger of shit, semen and piss.

In the middle of the open field Lieutenant James Bradley and Private August Huebner watched Gentle. They lay on their sides, elbows propped up on their bedrolls. Lieutenant Bradley let his mind wander back to the morning before, when they left to scout around the Little Bighorn River.

The night before the Crows were the only ones who had any idea what had happened to Custer and his men. Some of the Crow Indians had been out looking around. The battle had taken place on their land. They were worried for their own. When they returned, they were too upset for Bradley to make out what they'd seen. Had all the Sioux really left? Major Reno's men on the hill said they'd begun riding off at Gibbon's approach. Spoke of it with wide eyes, with the credulity saved for miracles. Some of Reno's men cried on the shoulders of their comrades in relief.

But where had the Sioux gone?

Lieutenant James Bradley, as the leader of the first scouting party, was to set out at dawn to find out. Bradley didn't sleep. He had counted heads, both battle-ready and wounded, then reported to command.

At dawn he had called Huebner away from a sloppy morning cook and coffee fire.

Bradley stood talking with some of the Crow Indians that were part of the scouting party. One was crying. When Huebner caught Bradley's attention, the Lieutenant turned away, toward the rising sun, shading his eyes with his hand.

Bradley liked the tall, gangly German. He kept his mouth shut and could go forever.

We know they're out there, Bradley said to Huebner, we just don't know where.

The Indians?

Them too.

Hey, Cap'n, someone said.

He was set off from the straggly group by the fire.

What have you heard of Custer, sir?

Bradley didn't answer him, just took Huebner's arm, started to lead him away, but the speaker had stood up in their path. He wore tattered denims with his uniform bluecoat and the brim of his hat pinned back. A faded blue bandanna tied round his dirty neck. The wind was already kicking up dust, blowing it in their eyes.

What's the big secret around here? he asked. We all saw what them Injuns did to Reno. Why ain't we talking about it? What in the hell are we going to do? Wait out here to they come back and kill us all?

What's your name, soldier?

William Ezekial Gentle.

Where you from?

Wilkes County, North Carolina.

That's up in the Blue Ridge, ain't it?

So?

Would you rather come with us?

No disrespect, sir, I jes don't like sitting around here. Not after we lost all them boys on the Reno hill yesterday.

Well c'mon then. By the way, my rank is Lieutenant not Captain.

All the same to me, sir.

Lef-tenant?

The sound of Huebner's voice brought Bradley back to the present. In the waxing blue of dusk, they sat and watched Gentle.

What's he doing?

Killing flies, looks like.

Did you see him in the field with the horses?

How could I miss it?

He lost his head. That was no way to act.

Huebner picked a nit from behind his ear and squished it dead between two fingers.

They were hurt and suffering, Bradley said. Somebody had to do it.

There's a way, certain way to do things, right.

We'd like to think so most of the time.

What do y'mean by that?

I'm not sure, soldier. I think I'm learning some things though.

Bradley spit into the dirt and rubbed it in with his hand.

He must of shot at least five of them inside of a minute, Huebner said. He disobeyed your order.

It wasn't my order.

Huebner looked the Lieutenant over, more curious than surprised at what he was hearing.

He lost his head, Lef-tenant.

Maybe.

He was out of control. He disobeyed the Captain Jenks. They've flogged others for less.

Maybe. I spect they won't be doing any flogging for whatever happens for a few days.

Some birds had come up, and as he spoke Bradley watched them light on to some crumbled bread too mealy for any of the soldiers to stomach. One, then two sparrows. The first sun rose purple.

Maybe he jes did something the rest of us would have like to find a way to do, Bradley said.

What? Kill a bunch of defenseless, suffering horses?

I don't know. Kill something.

Bradley grabbed a handful of pebbles and tossed them at the birds. They lit out for the rising sun.

Gentle took off his clothes and walked in his drawers to the river. More birds shot up from the willow thicket, but he walked right on through them.

I guess he's going for a swim, Huebner laughed.

He's a good un.

And we're taking him with us?

We'll need his shot.

God help us.

They watched Gentle splash straight into the cold river. He strode in up to his waist then dove toward the bottom, a shadow-figure in the dark water, light now up in the sky but not yet down in the valley. In a few moments others joined Gentle and soon there were at least fifty men, washing themselves down in the river.

Bradley still felt the nervous tingling in his joints and stomach he'd had all the past day and it hadn't gone.

That Gentle reminds me of certain horses we used to have on the farm back home in Richmond, he said. Most of em would act like to please the humans. But a couple just stayed horses.

What did you call them?

Just horses, I guess.

Bradley watched his hand trembling as he spoke. When he caught Huebner's eye he held on to the ground to stop the shaking.

It wasn't that they couldn't be broke, he said. It was more like they didn't know what broke was.

Huebner packed a pipe with the litter of stems and odd leaves that stood in for tobacco in the regiment, lit it and passed it to Bradley. A swirl came up and carried the smoke away toward the to-morrow they were reluctant to begin. The wind rolled over tall grass in yonder field. They watched over the hundreds of restless men, soon back to themselves after the quick respite in the water, restless shadows on the hillside. The two passed the pipe, and in this manner gone were the last minutes unto dawn.

When the dawn came they were still there, this, despite their prayers and oaths to the contrary. Private August Huebner got a good look around at the valley where they'd made camp. He re-membered just a couple days before, riding down through the hills with Bradley and Gibbon at the head of a long, proud column. Be-yond the river the mountains rose and there was the plateau Reno's men had retreated to. He'd never seen suffering like what had been up on that hill, the ones that had made it to the makeshift field hos-pital. Further along the ridge to the west was where they buried Custer's Seventh Cavalry dead. They'd found most of them down along the coulee ditch. The mountain ridge above them was bare, some sagebrush and brown grass, the water of the Little Bighorn River unbelievably blue.

They had done as much as they could for the dead, now they had to tend to the wounded. Those who had slept awoke now to their moans. Major Reno's men were spread out along the hillside directly above their riverside spot. Most had been sedated by morphine. Now they needed more. Colonel Gibbon detached some men to the willow thicket to cut down branches and construct litters for the wounded to take them down to the Bighorn River proper, where they could be transported by boat back to Fort Peck. There were only three doctors in the entire troop. They set broken bones, salved and wrapped wounds, dug out bullets with fire-blackened knives, gave out others to bite.

The sun never faltered, heat lingered into the afternoon, any breeze just blew dust at them. Corporals Bostwick and Goodwin volunteered and were commissioned to ride on to the Bighorn River to notify the Commander, General Terry, about what had happened. To tell them to be ready at the riverboat for their coming.

Bradley, Gentle and Huebner also set out.

Y'all circle around, the acting Commander Gibbon said, see if ya can git a trail and find where those Indians went off to. We don't need any more surprises. We ain't in what ya would call fightin' shape.

The three scouts rode right up over the rise then down through the coulee. They put their hankies back over their faces as they skirted by the field of the dead. They set their horses to a gallop and followed an obvious mile-wide trail that led away from the site of the abandoned Indian encampment beyond the river to the south. They saw no Indians, whether alive or dead.

What Indians had fallen they'd taken with them when they'd gone. Burned black earth and grass was all that was left. Near the southern end they found something.

Look at this, sir, Huebner spoke up.

He pointed to a series of calfskins left stretched over poles stuck in the dirt. They were hid from view by a clump of cottonwoods and a mess of sticker bushes.

What the hell is that? Gentle wondered.

Something.

I can see that.

It's a sort of celebration, a religious thing, I b'lieve.

They had a party did they?

Oh, go to hell, Gentle.

I believe I just now left it, Gentle said, and spit in the dirt.

Bradley ignored him then and rode over for a closer look. There were at least ten of the altars. Tied to each was a piece of the shredded remnants of a Seventh Cavalry flag guidon. On a couple hung the decaying heads of their comrades.

Bradley took his hat off.

Jesus, Gentle said, I've had about enough of all this as I can stand.

Maybe we should just go, Huebner said.

They kicked their horses and rode. Gentle went over and snatched up one of the skins and stuffed it into his saddlebag. When it cooled off later in the day and the rains began, he would wrap the legs about his neck and let the rest hang down his back for a coat. They stopped down by the river after following a trail that set out from the site of the encampment, resting and watering the horses in a thicket of willows. When they first smelled the rain on the wind, they mounted and rode straight up a draw to the top of a rise. They could see lightning in the distance. They rode into a wall of rain that swept over the high prairie. The mile-wide tread was easy to follow. Grass eaten down as far as they could see, on and on, over hill and bluff, rolling like a great, dried river current.

They chewed on dried salt-pork and hardtack. Bradley led with Huebner keeping back a step or two. Gentle rode in fits and starts, seeming to let his horse lead him, just riding its moods. He had an ungelded black stallion with white boots. He came back with it one night when they had camped on the plains. It was one helluva horse.

After a few hours they stopped at a fork in the trail.

Sir, Gentle spoke up, I don't think this is the right trail.

Private?

This looks older. This looks more like a coming trail than a going one.

Why do you say that?

I don't know. I jes do.

Huebner silently let his horse follow the other trail off a few steps then came back.

You think he's right? he asked.

It's hard to tell, Bradley said. A few days here or there.

This very well could be the trail they come in on.

Sure were a hell of a lot of them.

If this is the coming trail, they come together right here.

All we ken do is follow this un, see what we find and then try t'other.

How will we know?

We won't, Gentle spoke up. There ain't no way a knowin.

If we find em we'll sure know that.

From the highest rise they could look back to the soldiers' campsite and watch the rain on its way.

Hell now, Gentle said, for what it's worth, I'm glad to git away from all that back there. What you say there, German man?

You can call me Gus. Anyway naw, I don't think anyone ken fault ya that.

Maybe the rain will help.

It would take a helluva lot, Bradley added.

The three riders camped in the rain that night under the cover of a bluff of dripping cottonwood trees. In the dead of night Huebner awakened to a pitched whining sound. A horse? The wind? Gentle was grinding his teeth in his sleep. Huebner had some bad dreams himself. He went for a walk and skipped stones across the black water of the river. Once he got six skips.

They set out again in more rain the next morning, shared a ration of coffee between them, nibbled hardtack. Rain hit them in waves. They rode through clear blue skies, turned gray by the hour, clopped on through mud and splashed through puddles, rode up rises, down cuts and along the stark, jagged edges of the coulee-ditches. Hours passed, the country unwound and so did they.

You see any Indians? Bradley asked Huebner.

No, sir. I sure don't.

They stopped by an exposed stone face, burnt red and white shale, pink aged striates in the rock. When they stood still the day had a silent quality to it, as if for a moment there was no sound at all, then up would come the crickets and constant wind.

They're going to want us to have seen Indians.

I know it. I call em as I see em.

What if they all just split up?

Say what, Gentle?

That's what I woulda done. We're the ones that gone and brought the fight on. You're the Indy-ann expert.

So?

You said there were different tribes on the battlefield, right?

The Crow guides said mostly Sioux, Comanche and Cheyenne, Bradley answered.

What were all of them doing together like that? Gentle asked. I mean besides whipping our white asses.

Bradley took a drink from his skin then looked off through the rain.

Maybe they only got together to lick us, Gentle went on. I heard some of the boys talking before, said their chief done gone to soldiering school.

Ta-tanka I-yo-take.

What say?

That's Sioux for Sitting Bull, Private.

Ya ain't got to show off now. They could be in the mountains watching us now. They could be miles away.

Your counsel is well-taken, Private.

Ahh hell, don't talk to me like a kid. I could be as right as anyone. I'm serious.

So am I, Private Gentle.

Bradley looked at Huebner, who remained silent.

In any event we will double back toward the river. We can pick up the other trail then head down to meet the rest of the troops.

They rode on through a series of great desert bowls set between the rounded buttes, one after another that turned the day into night. This was out in the open with the sun burning the wet off the grass. As they rode in the dark the rains came once more. They kicked their horses and hurried on. They hoped to make it before midnight.

But they rode up to the river, well into morning and came upon the soldiers making their last tramp to the waterside. Private Huebner saw a man kneeled down with his head in his hands off by himself by a cottonwood tree. He got off his horse, went up, offered him his canteen. He heard what they'd missed while they were gone.

Everyone who could helped to get the fallen men to the river. They had started with two men per, carrying litters fashioned from cut saplings, but in the slicing rain and sticky mud they needed four and sometimes five. This man, a Private Nick Edelson, was helping to pull his brother's litter. The Edelsons were Jews from Kentucky. Brother Jack had been wounded through the stomach by an arrow in the first exchange the week before on the Rosebud with General Crook. His brother saw him; they were shooting side by side behind a wall they'd built of mud and rocks for the charge of the Indians. He went for a doctor, but returned with only sympathy to find Jack with the arrow in his hand, a tight grimace on his dirty face. He'd bled horribly that day and even now, after being bandaged and dressed, two days later.

Nicholas stayed with his brother. Men on the march had fallen numerous times and often poor Jack had fallen to the ground. He never complained, and was humble toward the men he was so dependent on. His moaning was constant. When after a fall it stopped, the elder Edelson was dead. For a while his brother wouldn't leave him. Finally, he did. He said a prayer, took his brother's personals and went to catch up with the troopers. Broke his heart to leave him like that.

After a five-and-a-half-hour trudge, the troop had only made it four miles. Under the General Crook's orders they stopped and made mule litters until dusk.

The line spread out. Stragglers arrived at the river throughout a sad and rainy night. The soldiers made it to the river in miserable rain and pitch-black dark to load the wounded on the riverboat called *Far West*.

The officers were drinking. Their tent reeked of wet horses, of tobacco, corn liquor and the men themselves. Old Crook was there, with long beard wound into two points with candle-wax, stained brown from his constant pipe. He hobbled around, declaiming all the finer points of why he was still alive and Custer dead. When the scouts came in, he sat down and hit off a tin of strong black coffee. They said he never drank. Gibbon stood by with a quiet intense drunk on. He bit the bark off a stick, watching the approach of the three scouts when they rode up out of the darkness. One hand on the pole for steady, cigar chomped in his teeth, bottle on his thumb.

The three scouts tramped through the night's relentless rain. They tied their horses to a cottonwood tree by the black rushing water then clomped through ankle-high mud. Private Gentle lost a shoe and cursing had to pull it out of the thick muck. Gibbon greeted them solemnly, squeezing Bradley's shoulder and then Huebner's, nodding warily at Gentle's cock-eyed grin. The Private, a bit cowed to actually meet the command, just stuck the boot back on.

Reno also came up to greet them.

Boys, boys, boys . . .

His voice was high and reedy, a dog stuck under a fence. He hit off a tiny medicine bottle of morphine, walked with a limp. Bloodless face pale as his white beard.

You boys been . . . you boys been . . .

He huffed twice, leaned back with an empty fish-eye smile. A horse stuck its nose through a flap in the tent. Reno walked toward it and held the empty medicine bottle to one of its nostrils. The horse snorted and he patted its nose.

You got to excuse Major Reno. He ain't hisself just yet, Gibbon said and led them in.

Gibbon ladled out bowls of stew for each of them as thanky's were exchanged by all. Next to Gibbon was Terry, a very courtly gray-haired officer, and the two of them made quite a contrast to the earthy Crook and Reno. His uniform looked newly pressed even out here in the mud and rain. Bradley'd never seen the man when he didn't look immaculate. He had on his full dress blues, even down to the white gloves.

So tell it, Gibbon spoke up. What did you boys find out? They out there?

We did follow some trails, sir, Bradley answered. Saw some real strong signs.

But you didn't see any?

No, sir.

Gibbon stuck one end of his stick in his mouth and chewed, thoughtful for a moment.

Hellfire, he said. If we don't find some Godforsaken red men, after what happened to Custer we'll be lucky if they don't call us all home next week. We had three columns of men right there. If Custer'd a waited we could have got em right there.

Gibbon tossed the stick away, crumpled up his cigar, balled the leaves into a wad and stuck them in front of his teeth.

Damn right that, Reno said, and stood up.

They all turned to watch and to listen. General George Armstrong Custer told me to go in first and he'll foller, Reno said. He never come. That lying sumbitch got my best men killed.

Now hold on, Terry said coolly. He shook his head and turned back to Bradley. His manner was like the others hadn't spoken. Well, we want you boys to keep going, that is if you're a willing to.

Terry smoked his tobacco in a pipe and drank his liquor from a glass. Bradley couldn't tell he was drunk until he got up close and smelled his breath. Terry's manner was like that of a kindly father, waiting to be told an answer he knew himself. He placed one gloved hand on the Lieutenant's shoulder. He looked Bradley flush in the eye as he spoke to him, his crystal blue eyes taking his measure, drawing the soldier up to his full height of six-two.

We're counting on y'all to keep an eye on them Injuns. We got a score to settle.

Yes, sir.

We wouldn't want to miss the dance, Gentle spoke up.

Well now, Terry said, and laughed like he didn't mean it. I sure do like the sound of that soldier.

He patted Gentle on the back.

You got yourself a game crew there, Bradley.

Yes, sir.

We're going to need some time to regroup here, the General went on. But we'll be ready soon enough and we're going to count on you scouts to lead us to them.

We don't want a repeat of the other day, Gibbon spoke very quietly, but no one missed a word.

He had that draw, something about his eyes, watery and red though now, a witness that had seen something very important.

It is our opinion, Terry broke in again, that they've gone on to hide in the mountains. With this he looked off into the rain outside, flicking some speck of mud off his boot.

We should be ready in a few weeks, Gibbon said. He blinked his eyes and rubbed his brows. Bradley could only tell how drunk Gibbon was by how slow and measured was his speech, by how red were his eyes. Bradley's father had been exactly like that, on his Saturday bouts. His pa had him when he was an old man, his pension bride dying in childbirth. He'd start in on the bottle in his bath, the tub an old tin one in the middle of the kitchen, made the boy carry buckets of steaming water, dripping sweat from his forehead. Pa telling stories of his soldiering days. When he'd come in late from the bar, he would wake young Bradley and tell him stories in the blue light of dawn. He went off to war an old man and came back dead.

We'll set up camp at the Tongue River, Gibbon went on. When the new recruits arrive we'll be at full strength once more. Right, General Crook?

Yes, sir, Colonel, I've sent word for the Fifth Cavalry, with them to join the Second and Third, we'll have up to two thousand men. We'll be ready for those Sioux next time, boys.

We await your orders, Bradley told the command, nodding at each respectfully. We are ready to ride.

Sometimes the old man would slap him, not hard, just so you'd be ready when the time comes, ready for the things his dad always spoke of, women, fate and heaven, ready to be brave. He always had to be ready, the slaps would come out of the blue.

Well, tell me this, boys, Terry said, turning on his heel to face them all again. Can y'all be ready to go in the morning?

Yes, sir, we could leave now.

Well, finish your dinner, at least. Terry laughed his breezy laugh. Get some shut-eye and leave in the morning.

Have a drink then, boys, Reno spoke up. Up and reeling, his eyes almost shut, hand in his pants, scratching obscenely, the other gripped a fresh bottle of rye. Would have run straight into Gentle, if he had not gracefully stepped back and accepted the bottle, drank and passed it around. Huebner stepped up, caught Reno in mid-reel. The Major leaned on him as he spoke.

What's your name, son?

August Huebner.

Have a smoke?

When Huebner graciously accepted, Reno handed off a cigar and turned to Gentle.

And you?

William Ezekial Gentle, Private that is, Third Class.

Good name, the Major nodded. Bible name. Tell me now. Are you scared of the Lord, son?

They all watched Reno as one might a horse in the middle of a fall, to see how bad it might be.

No'm.

You ought to know now, son. If y'are or not. You ought to know.

Yes, sir.

Behold, the princes of Israel, Reno blinked his eyes and recited, every one were in thee to their power to shed blood. Son, do you know that verse?

Why it's from the book of my namesake, sir. I knowed the whole thing. It's how I learnered how to read.

Can thine heart endure, Gentle recited, or can thine hands be strong in the days that I shall deal with thee? I the Lord hath spoken it.

Reno took Gentle's hand and led him through the tent flap out into the drenching rain.

C'mon, son, he said, let us go out into the rain for a moment.

Everyone looked at each other, one by one then at their feet. Crook's mouth was wide open. He nodded at Gibbon, who just shook his head. In a moment the strange pair were back, rain running off the bills of their hats.

All right then, boys, get what sleep you can, Crook stepped up. Come by and see me before you go, Lieutenant Bradley. We'll settle it all out.

Gentle, with Huebner's help, very kindly and indulgently led Reno back to his cot. The Major whispered in Gentle's ear all the while, as the Private nodded quietly. After salutes all around, the three scouts walked back out into the rain.

What did he say to you out here? Bradley asked.

He wanted to kneel and say a quick prayer, sir.

I'll be damned.

3

The three scouts left again in the deep blue just before dawn. Rain lay heavily on the leaves of the cottonwoods and wet their faces. A flock of white birds led them over wide open pale gold grasslands. Bradley had dreamed of his father, sleeping fitfully. The weather broke for a few hours and though it was still cloudy, a teasing purple-edged sun peeked over the great and distant mountains. They rode toward it. They circled the river valley, skirted the edge and headed west onto the high plains.

Major Reno had insisted on giving his new friend Private Gentle a full bottle of rye and evidently Gentle and Huebner spent the last of the evening drinking. Huebner, for one, could drink whatever was put before him. Bradley had seen it before. Now Bradley watched as the gainly Private Huebner spent most of the morning bent sideways throwing up off his sturdy bay. He never stopped, nor did he look embarrassed. Gentle still looked drunk, his eyes swimming in their sockets, his body lurching in the rolling rhythm of his horse's gait. Gentle talked to his own horse as they rode, often openly gesticulating with his hands a particular point.

There had been some provisions come along with the boat,

though Bradley noted that it hardly looked like enough for any extended campaign. Alone for a few minutes in the humid night, the Lieutenant brushed down his horse and went over his outfit. He had bridle and halter for his mount, picket rope and pin, nose bag and a bag of oats. In holster he carried a Colt .45, in the sling hung from his saddle a '73 Springfield rifle. His saddle was the McClellan with quarterstraps, girth billets and a heart-shaped safe. Strapped to its back a coarse wool blanket. He checked for the spare blue corduroy trousers and other essentials in his side mailbags. He unwrapped his officer's manual from its worn leather cover to note his provisions. When he licked his pencil, the taste of the lead on his tongue reminded of the fore-day's dead.

Most of the troops had been at work through the night loading the wounded, with the Generals Terry and Crook and Major Reno getting on last. Bradley had watched awhile then went off to find a place to lay out his bedroll away from the bustling and crowded riverside. He could not believe how tired the men looked, but then no one including himself had rested really since they had left their respective forts in May. What was just six weeks ago, seemed like six years. When the riverboat cast off, the three were all alone.

In the afternoon Gentle sighted a wildcat, on a rock maybe ten feet shy of a bluff of windblown juniper trees, shot it clean and galloped over to inspect his kill. When the other two rode up, walking their horses to give them a breather, there he was, cutting the creature's eyes out with his buck-knife. He cut them out as one would berries from a bush and popped them into his mouth.

We didn't need that for food, Bradley told him.

Huebner threw up again off his horse, a thin milky stream that splashed on his boots. When he was done, he struggled down off his horse and kneeled to wash his face from a clear blue water-lie.

Yeah, Gentle answered, still chewing, calm and strange.

He'd gone somewhere faraway. He looked off. Dark gray clouds ran along the high plains to the north, too low for rain, like they went all the way beneath the ground. Dark for miles in the distance, the smell of wind. Gentle gutted the animal, wrapped it in the Indian calfskin and slung it to his saddle.

We got some food offa the boat, y'know, Bradley said.

A man sometimes needs some fresh kill, Gentle said.

In the late afternoon the sun began a slow descent toward the distant blue-peaked mountains, and they stopped in a field brilliant with wildflowers, a carpet of yellow, white and purple. The horses slowed when they first stepped down into it, suddenly from over a hill. The flowers filled up the entire valley with their bright color and soft scent.

Lookit there, Huebner pointed, speaking his first words of the day. He looked over at Bradley.

Why don't we stop here then, Bradley said, and they dismounted. The German liked to study the flora. He would keep samples and record them dutifully in his notebook. Huebner crouched to pick a bouquet of the six or seven different varieties right there at his feet. He seemed a little embarrassed in front of Gentle, but he kept on. After a moment he stopped, looking off toward the far-off cloudbank.

Private, what are you worried about now?

Well sir, if you don't mind my saying. Looks like a storm up ahead.

That storm's at least a half-day's ride on.

I was jes' saying . . .

There is quite a constant breeze out here.

Begging the Cap'n's pardon, but that ain't no breeze, Gentle said, walking up and wiping his mouth, startling them both. He spit, but his mouth was dry.

Do you know the names of these? Huebner asked Bradley.

Naw, Gus, they're all weeds to me, pretty though.

I used to pick them for my mother in the morning, the German said. I could never sleep late. At dawn I'd go into the woods. I'd knock on the door and surprise her. Hold them behind my back.

What a sweetie, Gentle kidded. I bet your old mama misses you now.

She's been dead for a long time.

Gentle hung his head. They were all three quiet, just the wind and the rustling country sound of the horses pulling the grass from the ground with their big teeth. The three scouts lay out on the grass under a suddenly open and sunny sky.

It looks like those purple clouds might just lay down and fill up this whole valley, Bradley mused.

I know the names, Gentle said. He had walked off as always for a minute by himself, but now he was back to the other two. I know the names of those flowers.

Now do you?

Sure I does. My granny told me all of em. The yellers are yer Black-Eyed Susans, the purple is Indian Paint Brush and the white, Grandma's favorite, are called Queen Anne's Lace.

Those sound like Tennessee names, soldier.

Naw, I b'lieve they be same around—ahh, Cap'n, quit pulling my leg.

Hey wait a minute. Do you see what I see? Huebner pointed.

The Indians were maybe a hundred feet away. They were playing in the flowers, a squaw and her two children, in the grass with a puppy.

Have they been here the whole time?

Goddamn.

Bradley gave his horse's reins to Huebner, who dumbly handed him the bouquet of flowers. Bradley held them awkwardly, straight-armed, before him and started walking toward the Indians. When they didn't seem to mind, he called and then tried to talk a bit. The others followed cautiously. The woman wore a U.S. Army hat. She'd turned it backwards with the crushed bill behind. The crossed swords Seventh Cavalry pendant glittered in the sunlight. She had dark red skin, copper-colored but with a light that glowed in the sun. The kids played with the puppy's floppy ears, and scratched its white hairy belly as it rolled and tumbled around in the flowers and grass. Inside its tiny mouth the pink skin was freckled brown. Tiny sharp teeth just coming in.

When the Lieutenant offered the flowers, the squaw stared ahead warily. Bradley tried his rudimentary Sioux. She gathered her children to her and made to leave quickly, looking back over her shoulder as she shooed the children on. They just left the puppy.

Gentle picked it up, but then Huebner took it from him.

Hey, c'mon, he said, I like dogs.

Huebner just looked at him warily, careful. I seen what you done to them wildcats.

Gentle had this look, sorry-like, that he turned then on Bradley. The Lieutenant just ignored him. He was intent on watching the Indians. For Bradley everything disappeared except the woman, her children and the blue bummer's cap she wore on her head.

Does it matter? Bradley said. When they're out of sight, we follow them.

Really, fellas, Gentle said. I like dogs. Who doesn't like dogs?

Huebner smiled and looked at the ground. He put the puppy in his sack and started gathering up his book and flowers.

Gentle had followed him back to the horses.

C'mon, old Gus, you got to tell me, fella, you don't think I'm crazy do ya. I had a dog at home. I did.

The tall German finally took his shoulder.

We can share the dog, he said. No one thinks you're crazy.

Really! Gentle squawked. Do you think we can keep him? Sir?

What does it matter? Bradley said. Let's walk the horses for now, slowly.

Gentle scratched the puppy's chin and when it barked, Bradley glared back and then it was quiet.

The weather changed again. Clouds swirled in over them, lower and lower until suddenly the whole valley was dark. They walked their horses through clumps of prairie clover to the top of a sandy ridge and were suddenly enveloped by a bank of fog. They climbed the rise in the middle of it.

What the hell happened? Gentle said. Goddamn . . .

He put one hand out in front of him to feel his way, but it didn't help.

I can't see a damn thing, Bradley said.

They're still there, Huebner said. I can see them up ahead.

The Private concentrated on the last place he'd seen them. The clouds swirled, opening and closing like a veil.

Well, keep your eyes on them, Private.

Yes, sir.

Goddamn, Gentle kept saying.

He didn't like this, not one bit, reminded him of the blindfold games his cousins would play on him where they'd take him to the woods out by Dobbins Gorge for hide-n-seek, tie a hanky over his eyes then all just run off.

Just keep walking, soldiers, Bradley called. Maybe this fog will just let up.

But it did not. Before they knew, it was dark and even Private Huebner had lost sight of the Indians.

Damnit all to Hellfire, Gentle said.

They can't be far, Bradley said. You men can stop if you want.

If you're going on, then so are we, Cap'n.

All right, let's tie up the horses and split. They can't be far. Fog's got to lift.

They spent the night wandering lost, troubled to even keep track of the horses, passed the entire night on the same flat hilltop with no idea where they were. Gentle slept the last hours before dawn curled up with the puppy in the hollow of an old twisted cottonwood tree. He had panicked, calmed down again then finally gave up in exasperation. He just had to crouch there. Huebner walked up and down the hill and ended up lying down on a bank, hardly even able to see the earth underfoot. A few times he fell, sliding down the slippery shale-face of the rise on his knees, his boots or a few times, flat on his ass. Bradley couldn't stop. They were out there, and they were close. They had to be.

Morning sun burned off the fog. Down below lay the leavings and remnants of the village. The walls to the valley were exposed rock and red clay. A small blue water creek led through a patch of white cone-top wildflowers and some knife-like brown bushes, by a bank dotted with a wavy amphibious brush. The breeze blew them back and forth in waves like a water current. All the trees, mostly scrub pine and willows by the water, were broken off and scraggly. Beyond the flatbed stretch, long rocky steppes rose. They mounted their horses, kicked their flanks and rode careful, sideways down a thin pony trail.

They found lots of bones, and a pole flying a gold stripe torn off the pants of a Seventh Cavalry uniform.

Damn them, Huebner said.

They're fucking with us, Gentle said.

Bradley didn't say anything. He got off his horse and walked around the valley, once in a while picking at a clump of grass that had been left by their hungry horses.

Well, they ain't eatin too well, he finally said.

What kind of bones are those? Gentle asked.

They're eating dogs and they're eating their horses.

They ain't running from us, Gentle said. They're just looking for food.

You're probably right, Private. They have split up. This camp is nothing compared to what we saw in Bighorn.

What I think, they could care less about no war. They're just trying to get on like the rest of us.

'Ceptin' we won't let em, Huebner said.

Best not to think about it too much. We have our orders.

'Cept that increasingly I'm not sure how I like them, Gentle said.

Enough of that, Private, let's water the horses, find em some grass. Gus, it looks like your little friend is hungry too.

The puppy was yelping a bit, poking its head out of the side sack of Huebner's big bay.

In a few moments they rode onto the trail, Bradley in the lead. They followed it over rocky hills and humps in the earth, sagebrush and brown dry dirt, wild high grasslands, ancient bare rock shelves, down into dry riverbed cuts, between tall A-shaped buttes that made them feel small and tiny, red brown on top, coming stark and straight out of the bare, flat earth.

Gentle never really calmed down. Huebner talked to him, and let him ride with the puppy on his lap as he sat astride his horse. It looked very proud riding up there.

They followed the trail into the mountains. After a week their food was gone. They ate sour berries or whatever they could track and shoot. If it wasn't for Gentle, they would have starved. They rode through the heat of each day and camped in the dry cool of the night. They slept under the starlit sky on dirt hard as stone.

Bradley never lost his drive to find them again, to find something, anything. He insisted they keep their camp in perfect order, sleeping arrangements aligned with the North Star.

Isn't that a little weird, Cap'n?

I don't want to have to wake up and wonder where I'm at.

Huebner never really saw him sleep. Huebner never caught him. Suddenly Bradley's eyes were open and he was ready.

Gentle took care of the puppy, sharing with it the eyes from his kills.

Got to teach it who its friends are, he said.

The other two never saw most of what he killed. There'd be a shot and then Gentle riding off. As the days wore on he looked more and more ragged. Bradley worried about his health. Gentle wouldn't eat anything he didn't kill.

You look a little green around the gills, Huebner said to him once.

You ain't no princess y'self, German man.

Every other day they found another trail. They never knew what one meant. They didn't question Bradley, but his pace drove them raw.

The Indians fooled the three scouts with cold trails, into streams, to the edges of stark, dead drops. Once the three scouts came upon an arrow in the bed of a creek, fashioned out of snake skins and skulls.

I believe they are mocking us, sir, Huebner said.

They'll get theirs, Gentle said.

There was no more rain for now. Hot, unrelenting days, cold, unforgiving nights. They spent upwards of the month of July following the trail. Gibbon had told Bradley to meet them back at the Tongue River wash, the first week of August. On July Fourth they didn't even know what day it was. Huebner brought it up.

Today, I believe, is a national holiday, he said.

Well I'll be, Gentle said. Maybe we should least shoot off our guns or something.

Bradley didn't smile. He asked them to join him in a prayer for the fate of their country.

I'll pray for the land, said Gentle, but not for any Guvner-amint.

Bradley glared at him.

I just had to say what I had to. Man's a got to sometimes.

Sometimes I believe you just got to say too much, Private.

Aah now, all right I didn't say I wouldn't pray.

Huebner rode quiet as ever, stopping to pick flowers that were new to him, recording descriptions and taking samples for his notebook at night.

Gentle kept losing pieces of his uniform.

The three soldiers rode along steep mountain passes in a hailstorm where the scraggly desert met spots of solid ice. Sometimes the trail would split, or double back. They met dead ends, went on until they picked it up again. They subsisted on the hardtack boiled down into mush, on berries and ice and whatever they could find to kill, from rodents to snakes, even these tiny moles they came across once on the floor of a cave where they spent a night. Sometimes the trail broke off completely.

There must be ten different directions here.

I know it.

What are we going to do?

We're going to ride back and tell em what we found.

Do you think they're even going to listen t' us?

That ain't our concern, Private.

They sometimes sighted on smaller parties and then one day all at once the trails came back into one. They were on a long, wide plateau, swirls of cloud for company in the thin air.

Now they's back together. They's onto one trail agin.

Let's follow er then.

They headed back down the mountain now. They followed the source of the great Tongue River down. When there was no rain, the days left them in a constant state of wonder. Relentless beauty. Big blue cloud-laden skies they wanted to ride the horses right into. When it rained, no matter how hard or how long, they rode deep into each evening, following the pace of the other ones that were out there with them, sleeping for just a few hours each night.

One morning Huebner was watching Bradley. His eyes just opened. Huebner drifted off a little himself again, all of a sudden the fire was kicked over and the Lieutenant waited for them by the horses. A bright sun burned the dew off the grass as the two Indians came riding toward them in the distance. They could see them clearly from at least a mile off, across a valley to the next rise.

We got visitors, Huebner said.

He was the first to see the two riders. The puppy started barking and Gentle told it to just shush.

Don't pull out your guns, Bradley said.

Sir?

They wouldn't be coming like this if they weren't coming to talk.

Sir?

It's just not how they are. There'd be a lot more.

They put away their breakfast tins, scraped out the hardtack mash, cleaned them with the sandy dirt.

We'll mount the horses and meet them halfway.

They were quiet. Fifteen minutes' ride without a word.

When the two Indians were about a hundred yards from the soldiers, they raised their rifles and shot them off straight into the sky. Each loosed a piercing scream.

Bradley saw Gentle draw his rifle.

No, Bradley yelled. Don't! Gentle!

Gentle didn't listen. He squeezed off one shot and was loading the second into the trapdoor of his Springfield. Bradley felt the hiss of the bullet on his right ear. It was as if the wind had stopped, and all the other noises of the canyon, the buzzing flies, morning calling birds, everything. The horses bucked. The shooting broke the crisp yellow, green and blue beauty of the morning, like the devil walked into mass.

The first one fell, a burst of pink exploding from his ribcage. Dust rose and his horse started to walk around in a circle, dragging him by one foot. He hung upside down, obscenely, his loincloth flapped over his belly, genitals exposed to the sun and wind. The second horse took off at a gallop straight toward the three soldiers. They had not stopped; they were still walking their horses to the point where they all would have met. A growth of scraggly sagebrush jutted out of the parched earth.

Goddamn, Huebner said. He got em both.

Private, that was wrong, was all Bradley said, his voice quiet.

The horse with the wounded rider came on strong. Gentle had hit this one in the face, and weaving wildly, he clung to his horse's neck as the scared animal came on. Bradley turned back to Gentle. The Private dropped his third bullet and reached for a fourth.

You are against my order, Private. Bradley's voice rose.

Gentle just sort of growled and squeezed off the fourth shot. His face turned scarlet, a husky, raw sound emitted from his throat. His last shot struck the brave and sent him backwards over his horse. The horse pulled up, reared wildly. The Indian had been hit under his left eye and his face was already a mess of blood, brain and mucus.

Bradley's horse bucked now, pulling off wildly to the right, and he let it go. He had not foreseen this at all. He was a man that liked to be ready. It had all happened slowly. The sighting, the slow and solemn march of the two braves, their shots at the sky, and finally Gentle's part in it, then at once everything changed.

Huebner rode over to each of the Indians in turn. He untied the first one's foot from his horse and let him down gently on the ground, talking softly to the horse. He covered the dead man's loins. The horse sniffed for a few seconds over its former master then came to a stop and stood there staring.

Huebner slapped the horse smartly on the back haunch and yelled, Scat!

Bradley rode back to Gentle. The Private still held his gun stiffly before him. Bradley took the barrel in his own hand and the boy lowered it.

They raised their guns, Cap'n.

It was wrong, Gentle, you jes killed them, Bradley said.

Gentle breathed in and out slowly, wiped pouring sweat from his forehead with the grimy back of his hand. His mouth tasted sick and foul.

That's why we're out here innit.

His voice started somewhere low and mournful, but ended up almost angry.

We're out here chasing em ain't we. They killed our boys didn't they?

Dammit all to hell, Bradley said. What I'm worried about is what's going to happen when those horses get back to the rest of them.

You ain't a scared is you, Gentle got his voice back.

Do you really think that matters, Private?

Gentle just swallowed. He looked thirsty, like he needed to swallow, but he couldn't.

You got any water, soldier?

Nah. Gentle looked away, his hand up near his eyes, hiding.

Take some of mine.

Thanks, Cap'n.

Bradley spit, looking quickly to Huebner with the second Indian. The little dog sniffed at the bodies at his feet.

Do you have any idea how many Indians could be over that yonder hill?

Ah reckon a whole mess of em. What we gonna do?

We gonna head for the hills, find a spot and watch what happens.

They walked their horses up a steep rise, sweating in the heat. By the time they crested the rise, wails of the women carried in the wind. They hid in a deep wood area at the crest of the plateau. The sun set blood red over the valley and turned everything, the dirt, the grass, the jagged rocks, even the air, a pinkish tinge. From the cover of brush they watched the Indians retrieve their dead, gather quantities of wood, brush and grass. They built fires that as the sun set and the night fell filled the valley expanse with pulsating heat and light. Warriors stood watching the fires as squaws painted their faces in stripes and shades of red and blue. A cacophony of shouts, calls and singsong chants filled the vastness and echoed off the wall of the ridge.

Four men sharpened tree limbs and planted four-post scaffolds in the dirt and laid the bodies of the two fallen warriors atop them. Bradley and Huebner lay on their bellies on the cold earth. Gentle, restless even more than usual now, stood, then paced and finally sat a fallen tree trunk, stroking the puppy's head, whispering mostly to himself.

They had stood their horses back at the camp, and there by the edge of the ridge the three scouts felt alone and did not sleep.

The ceremony carried on until dawn showed purple over the rolling plains to the east. The bodies were taken down, placed on litters and warriors led a slow solemn procession up the very ridge of from which the three soldiers were watching.

I believe it might be time to break camp.

Try not to make any sudden moves. If they see us, we won't have far enough to run.

They made the horses, mounted and rode straight into the thickening wood. The songs of the mournful Indians filled their ears, quickened their hearts and haunted their minds for long after they had safely gotten away. They galloped their mounts through a series of long diagonal coulee cuts with steep bare earth rises on either side. When it broke into the open the three riders cut a trail through tall yellow grass that whipped against the flanks of their horses.

When they made camp, Gentle went off for a walk by himself. Bradley, Huebner and the puppy sat there before the fire when Gentle walked back up. He had a snake he'd killed, maybe four feet long. They watched as he cut its head off and let it bleed into his tin cookpot. He took out some part of the wildcat he'd kept wrapped up, all dried and blackened blood caked, added water, set it to boil. He cut a line on his forearm with his knife, and held it over the boiling pot.

Doesn't that hurt? Bradley said to him.

Gentle didn't answer. His face reflected the red coals, his forehead awash in sweat from the steam. The whole thing smelled like something from another world. Huebner watched, fascinated, stroking the sleeping puppy behind its floppy ears. It was brown with too-big paws and a snowy-white belly.

Bradley only watched now and then. It was unnerving though how little he seemed to care. He was writing the week's events into his journal, and studying maps. Gentle added a few drops of ink from his own jar. He dipped his knife in it and branded marks on both his biceps. Huebner watched him wince, once, then again. A cool breeze blew over them, carrying the sear smell of Gentle's flesh up and off. The young Private took a breath then started talking.

Do you know how old I am?

Does it matter? Huebner asked.

Naw, it's all right. Go ahead and giss.

You're already out here. Does it matter?

Please.

All right. I'll say twenty-one. I believe that is the regulation.

I turned seventeen last Christmas.

Well . . .

I just wanted to tell ya, that's all. Just in case.

All right.

There's something else, Gentle said.

He kicked at the fire, and all of them, Gentle himself, Huebner, the dog, even Bradley now looked away from the speaker to watch the coals skitter away into the dark, glow red fading to black.

My people is all dead too.

All right.

I ain't got no real papers. They jes took me in.

Private, Bradley spoke up. What matters is that you're a good soldier. Ain't no secret the way you look. Ain't nothin some of us haven't thought about. When I fought in the States' war, I wasn't much older 'n you.

You were there?

My father too.

Did you fight with him?

No sir, if he'd a known I joined when I did, that would been the end of it.

He didn't want you in the army?

Wanted me to go to proper college. When the war came and he was gone, I just had to go then.

You understand, Cap'n. I just had to say it.

All right.

There was an animal call, a wolf, more likely a dog or coyote, faint and far off, and the puppy lifted its ears.

All this ain't going to last, Gentle said.

Private . . .

We're in a bad place out here. Ain't no telling what it could do to any one of us.

4

In the morning they rode on, past patches of green cottonwood trees, and bare dirt flat-topped buttes, through knee-high brown grass and bright blue water swamps, over coulee cut stepped rises and rolling low-humped plains. Bradley checked his maps to send them on a roundabout trail back toward the Tongue River country where they were to meet up with Gibbon and the rest of the army. They became lean and hard from the weeks of riding, sinew, muscle and sunburned skin, rough as horsehair rope, dark eyed, taut of skin. Huebner and Gentle, even Bradley took off their blue coats and rode like braves, bodies exposed to the heat, wind and rain.

They could see the heat as they rode through it.

Their thoughts became like dreams, visions: vivid and in motion.

What they saw was slightly blurred, then clear and crystalline, with colorful trails, with shimmering light at the edges.

Dusty dirt, brown grass, deadish green sprouts rising in clumps
Pine and juniper
Badlands called by the Indians by the name Makoskika, or the stinking earth.

It looks like elephant skin.

How do you know what that looks like?

I ain't so stupid.

No one ever said you were, Private Gentle.

Turkey vultures

Agates: quartz crystal branches of brown and black

Fossils

They rode through the Pryor mountains, a remote highland junction of desert and ice with ice caves, limestone peaks and plateaus

Frenzies of wildflowers

Long straw-like grass with husky crests

Canyons, timbered hills, treeless plains

A blue river through a white desert

White crystalline waterfalls over mossy masked ancient rock faces

Rainbows over mountains in the distance

Sun-lit amber-colored land, sun-lit river water rolling like woman love-streams and climaxing over rocks

Bugs and rainbows, all shades of blue, green and brown, purple wildflowers, verdant long-lashed green grasses, rolling fields dotted with rocks, big distances

Like the clouds could come down and fill in the valleys

Human-like veins in land, land-like veins in humans, immense mountains always in background, watching

They're just fuckin with us.

So?

What do you suggest we do about it?

To hell with them.

Right.

We could shoot a bunch of em next time we see em.

That would be suicide.

You scared?

It would go against orders.

And that's important.

When you're a soldier, it is.

Hell, Cap'n Bradley, I'm just frustrated. Don't you feel that some-times?

Of course I do, Goddamnit.

I didn't know you could cuss.

That was for you, Private.

All hell. They could kill us anytime they wanted to.

Let's hope they don't.

Dry and cold, wrapped up and shivering in their blue coats by night, too hot and lashed to their saddles by day

Bradley prayed aloud every night, the Lord's Prayer.

Looking at the growing puppy he said one time: Y'know what I think, that ain't no dog, that's a wolf.

Can we still keep em? Gentle asked.

Gentle would laugh sometimes, uncontrollably, like an epileptic fit.

Huebner would be silent for days, taking wildflower samples, scribbling descriptions into his notebook.

If Gentle didn't know the names, sometimes on a good day they would sit together and make ones up.

Shooting stars: red budded stars, brown stem

Fairy slipper: wide opening mouth, pink inside of luminescent red

Lupine: purple buds falling up a brown stem, green leaves

False lupine: yellow series of buds

Finally in the month of August they made it back to the Tongue River to meet Gibbon and the troops. They rode out of a deep pine wood to the edge of a golden grass bluff and there were the troopers below. The soldiers' encampment stretched out for a mile over a wide open plain that led down to the blue river. Pale gray smoke from the supper cookfires hung in the air below them. It was late afternoon, a deep wine-brown and red sunset bleeding into the sun-scorched end of the day. Gibbon took aside Bradley to talk. When he offered his canteen, the Lieutenant wasn't surprised by the taste of liquor in the water.

Did you have any contact with them, son?

Well, we were approached.

When was this?

Maybe three weeks ago.

What happened, Lieutenant?

Well sir, Gentle shot them.

Gibbon's eyes widened and he took a drink from his canteen.

That would be that wild one, the young 'un. He shot em, did he?

I believe they wanted to talk to us, sir.

And our boy was not in a talking mood, now was he.

He disobeyed a direct order not to shoot, sir.

Well now, son, we won't hold that ag'in now will we?

If I may, sir?

Hold on. You can save that officer school stuff for the likes of General Terry. I'd rather you jes speak your mind with me.

Bradley took off his hat and wiped his forehead. The Colonel offered him another sip from the canteen and he politely accepted.

I like Gentle, but damn it, sir, he shot them Indians in cold blood. They hadn't raised their guns to fight.

And?

Well, sir, it just wasn't right. He jes killed them. He took it upon himself.

Bradley, I'm a little surprised to hear such sentiment from someone who spent as much time as you did out on Custer's field.

Sir?

I said surprised, not disappointed.

I guess maybe that's why I feel that way. Bradley looked straight at the Colonel.

You don't think what we're doing is wrong, do ya, Bradley? Gibbon held his gaze.

Sir?

Do you?

I'm a soldier.

I knew your father, son. Did you know that?

Yes, sir.

I was with him at Fredericksburg.

You was, you didn't see . . . ?

No, I wasn't there when he was killed, son.

Lieutenant Bradley swallowed, looking at his boots, scuffing a clod of dirt off them.

The Lieutenant looked over at a couple of horses, drinking from a pool in the bend of the river. The Colonel bent his knees, picked up some dirt. He squeezed and let the dry earth run out through his fingers.

Your pa wasn't scared of a fight. I know he'd want me to tell you he's proud of you, son.

The Colonel paused, caught the Lieutenant's eye. He held up his hand when Bradley started to speak.

And not only cause you're a soldier.

I appreciate your kindness, sir.

It ain't that, son. Now you want Gentle replaced or what?

Naw, I mean no, sir. He's with us. I certainly don't distrust him.

You mean he'll keep his gun pointed at the Indians.

Gibbon laughed loud and took a drink.

How old is that boy, anyway?

I believe he's twenty-one, sir.

You believe, hunh, that's a good un. Keep an eye on em.

Will that be all, sir?

Quit thinking so much, son. We're out here. All we ken do is make the best of it. Don't do nothing you don't want to. Then maybe you'll get out of here.

You mean alive?

I mean either way, son.

The army left the river camp at dawn. Never before or since had there been such a force in the west, with Generals Crook and Terry sharing joint command. The pack train and wagons that came in stead of the cavalries and the infantry afoot stretched for almost a mile. The soldiers to a man were tired and haggard, since winter in the field. The horses' bloated bellies flopped over their stick legs. They had only grass to eat for months. They foamed from their mouths and bled from their shoes. Every evening driving rain followed the lines into the dark.

Officers had no idea where the Indians were. Soldiers lost very quickly whatever faith they had in the leaders. Every day's plan, another fool's errand, another long muddy march. Bradley's scouts waited for orders to make reconnaissance, but none came forth from command.

Hey, Gus, this foot soldier stuff gets old pretty quickly, don't it?

You complain too much.

I ain't complaining.

What would you call it, Private Gentle?

C'mon now, you got to play fair, iffin you want to be my friend.

I didn't know it was in question.

Desperate for shoes, some men took the sleeves from their shirts to wrap round them so they might only hold together. This made marching harder, but they needed something to cover their feet; they weren't savages. When there was not rain, the heat was tropical, humid and close. Their clothes never dried and in the early afternoon steam rose from their woolen uniforms. They smelled for miles.

Trailed by turkey vultures, batting off large biting black horseflies by light, mosquitoes by dark. Rainy reveille at six, breakfasts of water, and bitter, stale coffee. They marched twenty-five to thirty miles each day through the heat, then came more rain in the evening and frost by night. Within a month they were killing the pack-mules for food.

They crossed the Cannonball River into Dakota Territory. The terrain was uneven. They stepped in prairie dog holes and snake dens, in puddles and mud six inches thick. Land barren save cactus, nothing to drink from but alkali-spoiled waterholes. Nothing to burn but cactus and the long twisted grass. One day some cavalry saw Indians in the distance, but their horses didn't have it in them to give chase. They crossed more Indian trails. Their eyes burned, they coughed up blood. Men collapsed with their horses in the rain. The soldiers' line strung out for miles: tired, sore-boned, sick to their stomachs and their hearts. They cussed, complained and spit when they could; some just broke down and cried like girls.

After a month of this General Terry decided to break up his command. At a tributary of the Little Missouri River called Beaver Creek, he received word that the Indians had scattered. He sent Colonel

Gibbon's infantry back to Fort Ellis and Major Brisbin's cavalry to Fort Shaw.

We're losing more to the land than to the Indians, Gibbon said in a meeting with his scouts.

We'd like to go on with Crook, Bradley told him.

It's your funeral, son.

Bradley, Huebner and Gentle rode on with Crook through the valley of the Little Missouri. Still plagued by rain and short on supplies, the General decided to let the ration problem take care of itself. The men wondered what he could be thinking. Soldiers shot worm-rent, exhausted cavalry horses, three per battalion; foot soldiers had the mules. These animals offered little sustenance; they were gaunt and bloated. The soldiers were grim and silent, compelled forward by hunger.

The rain got colder, fog denser. They stepped on each other's heels. Fights broke out. They said things like:

Hell-Fire Louise.

Thought they said there was gold out here.

Must be buried pretty damn deep.

Just a bunch damn fools s'wut we is.

Crook remained tight-lipped and silent, mad with determination to find some, any Indians. He refused to give up and go back.

Every day the officers selected more animals to be shot and butchered. They turned their heads and pulled the trigger. When they reached the Grand River, Crook sent Captain Anson Mills south toward the mining town of Deadwood to get provisions. Along with Mills rode the 150 cavalrymen who still had horses.

Attack and hold anything red you come across, General Crook told Mills before they left, but don't expect support right away.

Bradley and Huebner rode with the main cavalry column. Gentle, sick to his stomach and vomiting, was left to remain with the foot soldiers. After so many months in the field, their blue striped pants and knee-length black boots were the only clothing that marked them as military. They were splattered from head to toe by mud.

Frank Brouard and a small detachment including Huebner spotted a Sioux encampment in the middle of the night, a small herd of ponies and fewer than forty lodges in an amphitheater indentation in the eastern edge of the Slim Buttes.

Mills decided not to wait. They would leave their livestock in the hills and ride down at dawn, try to surprise them sleeping. He selected twenty-five mounted soldiers for the charge, Bradley and Huebner among them. The others surrounded the camp on both sides. The object being to stampede and capture stock while killing as many warriors as possible.

That night it rained. Dawn found the soldiers slogging through mud into a deserted village. The Sioux, hearing their approach, had fled south through the only open flank into a deep-cover ravine. The soldiers sacked thirty-seven empty teepees, with a Private McClinton finding a cavalry guidon from Custer's command. They dodged bullets that came hissing up out of the ravine. They heard taunts, barking like dogs and chirping like birds. They could not see them. A Private named Wenzel, spitting mad and screaming like hell, charged down the creek bank. He was shot in the nose. In a flank attack one shot hit Sergeant Kirkland in the side, another shattered Sergeant Glass's left arm. A Lieutenant named Philo Clark led twenty volunteers who were chased away, yelping like dogs, with not a single shot fired. It was a complete standoff when Crook arrived with the rest of the army. A dense thicket of cottonwoods and steady stream of rifle fire kept the soldiers on the hill above the ravine.

Well, damn them, we'll just have to shoot till they come out a begging, the General said.

The shooting started after the soldiers had their fill of what food the Sioux had left.

Privates Huebner and Gentle took their places in a long firing line above the canal.

Private Billy Gentle lay chest down in a mud dugout. A mist rain chilled his face and hands. He heard the voice of a child. And he heard birds. It bothered him that there were birds, but he kept shooting anyway. The baby crying didn't seem right. It was coming from deep down in the ravine. Now he was talking to Huebner. He tapped him on the shoulder, to say howdy. He felt his lips moving; he felt the words forcing out of his tongue. He knew what he wanted to say. Huebner even saw him talking through one corner of his eye; he turned an ear toward him. All Gentle could hear was the baby and the gunfire.

He wanted to tell the German about the voice, about the child. He must hear it too. Gentle had not seen Huebner or Bradley for almost a week now. They were chosen for the special mission. He wasn't. That was alright. At least the dog had stayed with him. The men took it on as a mascot. As it grew, its markings changed.

That ain't no doggie, one soldier said, that's a wolf.

Gentle got a bad stomach. He couldn't eat, sleep or shit for three days.

Huebner had his own problems. He couldn't hear anything but the gunfire anyway. He couldn't believe what they were doing. His gun kept jamming. He thought he came to fight in a war; this was slaughter. He'd shot four of them, two women, a man and a child.

One of the women was beautiful, with green eyes he saw clearly. Maybe he just imagined them; maybe he saw more because he was scared. He saw the woman before she saw him. She had a gun and he shot her. A brave with his face painted the color blue of a robin's egg propped up her body to shield himself. Her beautiful face, the green eyes that he saw were no more, were soon a bloody mess.

A bullet hit Gentle in the leg, just above the knee, felt like a hammer on his muscle. It locked up. He didn't want to stop, or tell anyone about it. This would be his secret for now. The pain helped. He didn't want to give it up. And he was scared of the morphine. He'd seen what'd happened to the others. The desperate, begging sweats between doses, the wide-eyed nightmares. He was scared someone might cut off his leg. When he was a kid back in the Blue Ridge, he'd known a man in his town who had no leg, whose pants hung over a stump. That one word stuck in his head. He thought it must have looked like a tree, chopped right off, with rings, dripping sap.

Private Billy Gentle took off his bandanna and bit it down with his teeth. He wondered where Bradley was. He'd seen him before with the officers, talking, looking over his shoulder. Bradley had caught his eye and winked. He missed Bradley most of all. It wasn't fair that they'd been separated, after he'd gotten used to them like that. What if the Lieutenant were hurt, lying somewhere, and needed him? He thought he loved him now. What if he up and died like the rest had back home? Gentle wanted to go and look for him, but he couldn't move, what for his knee, what for the voice of the child in the ravine. He wanted the voice to stop; he wished it never would. He wanted it dead. He wished the kid was off somewhere in the wild, where he couldn't hear it, where it belonged. A place he wished sometimes he'd never seen.

Lieutenant James H. Bradley stood watching him from behind the line. He saw the blood, darkening the private's pants. Before he knew it, he had tramped through the knee-high grass to be with his men.

Gentle! he shouted. Huebner!

Bradley had to grab Gentle's shoulder and shake him.

Gentle at first just jerked back once, like it was some small bother, a fly in his ear. When he turned full, his gun pointed at the Lieutenant's chest. He still had his finger on the trigger. With the other he reached for the safety cock. They both heard the click.

Goddamn, Cap'n, he shouted. Give a man some warning next time. What's up? Come to git ya some?

Bradley shook his head.

Are you all right? he said. You been hit.

Don't ask me that, sir. Not now. Jes don't.

Bradley heard his name called and turned toward the sound of it.

Crook stood twenty yards away, picking mud off his boots with a stick. He stood under a white ash tree. The leaves dripping softly, audibly, onto the bare dirt ground.

Bradley nodded to Gentle and ran over to the General.

That's your boy.

Yes, sir.

He's been hit.

He's all right.

He's taken the bark off'n that tree anyways.

Sir?

Boy's been shooting straight at that ol' cottonwood for five minutes going. Wait, oh yeah now he's back after em.

Sir. How long are we going to keep this up?

Son?

This shooting, sir, how long?

I ain't seen no white flag, have you?

They'll all be dead.

I guess we got enough ammunition. Hell, it's the first we've used.

Jesus . . .

Yeah, son. It's a helluva way to do it.

Bradley nodded, snuck a look back at Gentle, and saw Huebner next to him. Gentle was trying to tell Huebner something.

Gentle's words were lost again, somewhere between his mouth and Huebner's ear. He imagined the ground was trembling. He'd never felt so hot in all his life. He wiped his brow and turned his head to the side for a moment. When he threw up, it felt better. Between the bullets, the pain and everything else, it's a wonder the whole mountain didn't burst apart, a wonder God just didn't take them all straight down to hell. He felt like he could cry, but he didn't want anyone to see. When he was a kid, and the others beat him up and left him behind the barn. Sometimes he sat there for hours.

The shooting into the woods took most of the night into the next day. It was dawn, the day unnaturally gray and smelling of sulfur from all the gunpowder, when the ones left alive started to trickle out.

Gentle thought the child was talking to him. He could hear its voice. The child spoke like it knew him, like they were friends. He saw a hillside with a stream and fish gliding silver through the water. The Indian child was there, waving to him across the water. He had caught a grasshopper in his tiny hand. He held it up to Gentle. He smiled and pointed at the fish. Gentle kept squeezing the trigger of his gun. He reached with his free hand to his leg. He rubbed the bad place to make it hurt. Sweat dipped down his forehead into his eyes. He took off his hat, shut his eyes and said, Jesus.

Gentle was mixed up, like he could see the voice of the child now and hear the looks on the faces of the Indians he was shooting at.

The voice of the Indian child stopped before he knew it was gone.
And later when of a sudden it was over and the hurt, angry, dirty,
bleeding defiant Sioux were walking out, the maybe ten what could,
he saw a kid, maybe five, a tear-streaked dirty, bloody face, and he
wished it was the one he'd heard. He wished he wasn't one of the
dead ones left there to rot amongst the leaves and dirt. He talked to
Huebner about it later, who said, Maybe dead would a been better.

The ten were left to be taken prisoner, including the Chief, American Horse.

Gutshot, he came out holding his entrails in one hand, and shook
Crook's hand with the bloody other. The General wiped his hand on
his pants only after the Chief had turned and limped away. American
Horse died that night, off in the dark away from the others, unap-
proachable, alone.

Later, soldiers went into the ravine to look around.

A bugler they all called Painter Joe Andoe saw a women so pale he
mistook her from a distance for a white man.

There's white folk in there, he said.

If there is we'll hang em from a tree.

A cry went up.

What Andoe had really seen was a squaw with her neck torn away,
shot thricet in breast, twicet in each arm, her blood drained away into
the earth where she lay dead. He saw another dead of a fatal shot under the ear, shattering away the warrior's skull. Only his face was left,
masking blood, brains and bone. An old man, his chest just a bloody
hole, who died determined and grim.

Soldiers buried their own dead, left the Sioux where they lay.

When next day shots came from the hills, the few captives told
some of the Cree mercenaries it was Crazy Horse and Gall, Sitting
Bull to come. Some soldiers believed them. Others said they were

just trying to scare them. Most of them just wanted to go home any-way. They rode south toward Deadwood. On the retreat they skir-mished all day with the Indians. That afternoon Bradley climbed a hill as fog and smoke cleared to watch them ride off into a gray mist. That night they huddled round a thousand campfires, ragged, cold, weak, starved, desperate; wild-eyed and raw of feeling from two days of carnage, death-fear. They ate the Indian ponies and kept warm with their skins and blankets.

5

Out of the sun the wind blew cold. The sun set red over the buttes and cast a perfect crimson-toned shadow over the parade ground. The box tip shade of the tallest butte barely touched the faces of a ragtag band of Agency Indians crowding in front of the quarter-master relief shack, turning their already dark faces a dusky, glowing reddish brown. Bodies completely in shadows, mismatched clothing no one else would have. MacKenzie's men kept a grim guard over the line. Reprimanded for brutality before with the Indians, they kept a close counsel. They were not happy, sharing quick nips from their hip flasks, and complaints about the cold.

Left of the square, still in sun, Private Huebner leaned against the unfinished adobe wall of the infantry barracks. If all went according to plan he would be leaving again in a week or two with Lieutenant Bradley's small detachment of scouts. For now he watched the Agency Indians as they straggled up to the window. The insulted and humiliated Indians took this chance to raise all kinds of hell, squawking in animal and bird calls, crowding up by the gate in a mob.

It'd been a month since the army had returned, broke-down, half-starved and pestilent from the so-called American Horse Victory

March. Although this month of November had been cold, there was sun. There had been some rain and hail too but as yet, no snow. In the butte canyon where the camp lay, the weather came on all of a sudden. It wasn't like out on the Montana High Plains, where they could see lightning bolts long before they heard the crackle of thunder and could track the progress of the storms across the sky. Here in the Dakota Territory there would be no warning, maybe just a sudden dark place in the sky or a hard breath of wind come over the buttes then suddenly it would sweep down upon them. Yesterday afternoon a drenching rain dropped big fat splashes of rain, turning the dusty parade ground into a welter of muck and mud.

It was the Indians' day of the week to collect their food, clothing and blankets. They'd come in since morning, by horse or wagon or foot, from their buffalo hide teepees in the hills, from mud and grass dugouts in the bluffs and from the stinking, infested, squalid quarters in the south end of the camp. Only the most depressed and desperate lived here in camp, the ones that had given up on any vestige of respect and veneration for their former ways. As dusk neared everyone else started to huddle for the cold as the sun threatened to finally disappear behind the distant buttes. Who had blankets wrapped themselves up. Most of these Agency Indians had not the festive blue, red and yellow colors woven of their former lives, but instead the drab scratchy green, gray or brown of the U.S. Army.

These Indians had been on this agency now for more than a year. Their land had been taken from them and this was what they were given in return.

Small wonder, Huebner thought, we have to chase halfway across the country to find them and that some of them would rather die. He saw an old woman, completely naked, her wrinkled paps more sickening than obscene, hanging just past her belly. She led by each hand two smelly children with their bellies distended and bulging past their impossibly skinny ribcages. The story went that both their parents had been killed, burned or just plain disappeared in a soldiers' raid in the fall, left to this poor old wretch. Maybe she was their grandma, maybe not.

All of them looked mad. The kids, also naked, played patty-cake behind the woman's back as she stood nealy-eyed, distracted, staring off into the sky. When Huebner could take it no longer, he grabbed his own blankets from his rack in the barracks and ran out to give them to the poor old woman, for herself and her kids.

She looked at him with wondrous confusion. She nodded, cutely, almost coquettish, and took the three blankets. This was when Private August Huebner saw the Crow Indian for the first time. He also came up to help the old woman. There was nothing said between the two men. The Indian handed over some shirts and food to her. Huebner got a good look at him before his politeness turned him away.

The Crow's black hair swept down to his shoulders. His face was painted the same color black over his eyes and outlined in white. A single painted tear fell from one eye. He was tall and barrel-chested with a big belly. He looked at Huebner and shrugged.

Huebner met the Crow Indian the next day. Lieutenant Bradley put him up to it.

Most of the men from the last campaign had been paid out their thirty-nine dollars for the three month campaign and sent back to their home units. Huebner and Private Gentle signed on again.

Where else am I sposed to go? You're going on, right, Cap'n? Gentle asked.

I am, yes, Bradley said.

Well, then, if y'all have me then I'm bound to go.

When the Lieutenant turned his gray eyes to Huebner the tall German just nodded. Working in the stone-cutter crews, laying down the roads with his back wasn't nothing to go back to. He hadn't anything, lessen to count the father he'd left drunk in the alley off the Raritan River docks back home in New Brunswick. He had gone to show him his uniform, but when he found him like that he just left it. Rode a stage to Philly where he caught the train for the West. Now he took off his regulation brown felt hat, a gesture that the Lieutenant took as a measure of the solemn nature of the moment.

I want you to know I want y'all both along with me, Bradley said. At the same time you should feel no obligation at all to remain in my command.

Ahh shit, sir, Gentle scoffed. G'wan with that. We sure do know what we're in fer.

When the Lieutenant laughed lightly and nodded back, Huebner took it as a signal to put his hat back on.

If ya don't mind, Cap'n, Gentle spoke up. I'm gonna get back to them drills. Them new boys they brought in since Custer are sorry.

They stood in the parade yard. A cold wind whipped leaves around their boots.

That'll be fine, Gentle. Uh, Huebner, can I have one more word with you?

Yes, sir?

This is important.

All right, sir.

You work with Gentle every day.

Yes, sir.

Do you think he's all right?

His leg's coming along fine, sir. Near as I can tell.

Huebner, I don't mean his leg.

You mean?

Yeah . . . is he all right?

You're worried?

I am.

About . . .

Don't act dumb. You know what I'm trying to get at, Bradley said. The Lieutenant chewed his lip. Now this is important too, he said. When we go. Should we take him with us?

No one else.

You're sure.

I trust him that way, for sure.

You're sure?

I trust him that way most of all.

One more thing, we got this new Indian Crook wants us to outfit as a guide, Bradley said. I want you to talk to him.

Huebner exhaled deeply. I guess I'm sposed to thank you for the duty, sir.

Don't, Huebner. It'll be good for you to learn.

I jes don't see what good those red-men do us.

The Gen'l thinks it's good for them. Teach them our ways and all.

So, he's a Sioux then?

Naw, he's a Crow.

I thought we'd lost all them scouts, after Custer.

So did I.

Do we know him? Is he one of our'n?

Sort-a. He was with Custer.

Huebner interviewed the Indian for the rest of the week. On the first day the Crow had offered him a drink from his water cup and Huebner said, Naw.

When the Crow just smiled, Huebner felt ashamed of himself.

The yard was always full in the afternoons with all the new arriving soldiers and Agency Indians. Most of the soldiers, as they arrived from their respective outposts, busied themselves with putting up buildings around the camp. The infantry barracks, erected just two years before, had to be shored up for the winter. A new officers' quarters was built out of adobe and sided with wood taken right out of the forest. There were two of the Red Cloud and Spotted Tail Indian agencies, these run by the government independently of the army as a way to feed and clothe the surrendered tribes until they could be shipped down to the new Indian Territory south of Kansas. When the Crow Indian Comes Up Red spoke all this seemed to drop away into the background.

Talking to the Indian reminded Huebner of his mother. She liked to take him to galleries, museums and exhibitions. He was maybe seven at the time, a boy in knickers and a brimmed hat, holding on to his mother's hand in the great crowds of New York City. After they would ride the ferry home down the river. When the Crow Indian Comes Up Red spoke of the world he knew, what was called wilderness by the white man, Huebner's mind would be drawn back to these days with his mother, to these days with the paintings. He remembered one by a Frenchman named Rousseau; the woods were dark and big, with a cut of red sunlight providing light only near the tops of the trees and the people in it, two humble women peasants, were very small, almost invisible. He remembered standing before them, clinging to his mother, jostled by the crowds that attended exhibitions in New York City or Newark that were held in the same halls where other days they showed prize cattle or once the circus of the great man, Barnum.

Another of the paintings was a depiction of an Indian encampment in the Rocky Mountains by a German immigrant named Bierstadt. It was at the Sanitary Fair in New York City in 1864, a show that lured in twelve thousand visitors a week. His mother had gotten for him a little picture book with a likeness of the painting in it and he had kept it long after her death, flipping the pages held up close to his tallow candle after the town had been given over to the night. It was one of the things that had led him out here.

The Indian never mentioned the day in the square with the old Indian woman, but Huebner knew he knew. He spoke little English, but after a few days they got along fine with the signs. The Crow had been there on the hill with the Seventh Cavalry after they'd split with Reno. Custer had called forth him and another Crow scout, to the tent they'd set up for him in the field, the white one with the red carpet set down on the harsh, dried and cracked earth. The General was getting his famous long blond hair shorn almost to his skull, sat there with hip flask in hand. Earlier he'd yelled at the Crows.

You're just a bunch of women, he said.

They had told the General what they thought about his plans.

To attack would be bad war.

The Crow scouts tried to make him understand how many Sioux, Cheyenne and Minnecoujou had gathered there in that Crow country in this time of the Great Sundance,

Iih-Wat-Xhao.

On night scouting runs they had seen many camps. Once they had actually snuck in amongst them and seen the great chiefs of the Sioux Nation, the medicine man Sitting Bull and the great warriors Crazy Horse, American Horse and Gall.

Y'all are just scared, Custer said.

He was trying to prop up his own troops. Most were fresh recruits, scared, tired and sick.

Just go on home, Custer told the Crows.

AMERICAN BY BLOOD   77

Afterward Custer walked his favorites, Hairy Moccasin, Bloody Knife and this one Comes Up Red, to the side.

G'wan, he said.

Hairy Moccasin told him they had chosen to stay and fight.

I want y'all to go to your fam-lies, Custer said. After I git done here killing these Sioux and Cheyenne—Custer paused and spat— I'm coming after y'all Crow. I'm giving you a chance here because I like ya, to save yer own.

He said that? Huebner asked.

The Crow nodded.

What'd ya say?

Then Comes Up Red touched his heart. He appreciated the General's honesty. He was trying to be true, in his own way.

Hell . . .

What is this? the Crow Indian asked him.

Huebner just laughed. The Crow waited. See those Indians over there, he pointed. They're in hell right now.

Comes Up Red nodded.

What did you do then? Huebner asked him.

He told Huebner that Bloody Knife stayed with the General. Then he pointed at his own chest and made a sweeping gesture of his arm.

I felt in . . . The Indian gestured toward the crowd.

In Hell, Huebner said.

Comes Up Red looked at him, then off for the sky.

For two days he sang, for two nights he dreamed. Hairy Moccasin went home back to his people. Comes Up Red was left alone.

Did ya see what happened, on the battlefield?

A big fire, the Crow said. Then he made signs for Custer, and made a throwing motion with his arms.

You saw him.

The fire, Yellow Hair.

We got there a couple days later, Huebner said.

The Crow pointed at his own eyes.

You seen us.

The Crow mimicked walking, and pointed off to the hills.

You left, Huebner said and spit.

Private William Gentle also had contact with the Indians, but it was of a different sort. In addition to other duties, he worked on interrogation of prisoners at the guardhouse. Captured Indians would be led out of the squat wood guardhouse in chains and shackles. Skinny, sullen, they wouldn't eat much of the food they were given. Gentle was struck much by their eyes. They never blinked. They talked a lot but said little. One day he took Huebner aside.

They sure do talk a lot of bullshit.

Do they now?

Wouldn't you?

Sometimes at night they howl like animals.

As veterans, Gentle and Huebner were given special duty, authority and most strangely of all, respect. Gentle and Huebner had killed. They'd been wounded. They'd survived. The story of Gentle's confrontation with the Indians out on the plain had been spoken of by soldiers and Indians alike. Besides the officers and a few others, they were also the only veterans of the Slim Buttes battle.

Gentle drilled the recruits as hard as he could, took a lot of pride in it. He knew why they were there. It wasn't about soldiering, like Bradley thought, or about uniforms and rifles to keep or extra pairs of pants. It was about death. They were all meant to die out there.

Some wouldn't, but they would have no control over whether or not. If they did live, the deaths they would witness, the blood, the gore, the frozen-in-death looks of horror and surprise would never leave them. What they witnessed would be in every grass-scented breath of wind, in every trembling leaf, in the eyes of every person they would ever say I love you to. The memories would come up upon them at odd times, from stray sensory connections, when they made love to women and held the warm bodies of their children.

One promise Gentle had made to himself that he remembered from after being shot up in Dakota was that if he lived through all this, he was going to have him about fifteen kids, as many as possible.

Gentle took the recruits through their paces every morning and noon. With his eyes slit, and a bunch of pebbles in his cheek which he spat one by one into the dirt.

Hup, hup, haw, he yelled.

Keep it in line, y'all.

Gentle wore his hat down over his eyes or back atop his head but never at the correct book-manual-described position on the crown of his head. He spent his spare time, his own time on the rifle range, or sometimes drinking with the MacKenzie crowd.

They're sure to be in the middle of the next fight, they all said.

He had heard through the ranks that Sitting Bull had run off on to Canada, that they were going back to Montana to get the one called Crazy Horse.

The officers had meetings and then more meetings. Private Billy Gentle often saw Lieutenant Bradley ducking in or out of one of them. Sometimes he got a wink from his comrade. Sometimes he did not. This time he waved.

Hey, Cap'n, ken a man talk to ya?

Yes, William Gentle.

That doggie we got.

Yes?

When we go out agin, I think we should leave him here. Where he can make a home for hisself.

All right, Private. Bradley scratched his head. Is there something else . . . ?

Well yeah, there is . . . them Indy-ans you got me talking to. They ken tell.

Tell what.

They know what we done up in the hills.

What are you talking about?

They gonna kill me.

Gentle, there's no way they could know anything.

Like hell, they know everthing.

We know the same about them then.

Hey, that's right. Damn, Cap'n, I hadn't thought about that. We got to kill them all . . .

Gentle . . .

Before they kills us.

William Gentle, maybe I should give you another detail.

My name is Billy. We done rode together and killed and seen God only knows what together . . . you ain't . . .

Look, Private. Gentle . . . Look at me. I don't know what happened to you out there, but you need to try to hold it in.

Gentle nodded, walking off a little.

I don't want no other 'signment, Cap'n.

Gentle, do you understand?

The Private just kept blowing on his hands out there in the cold.

I got you, Cap'n, he said.

Huebner went out walking one night, clear and so cold he could hear his steps crunch the cold frozen dirt. With a nip or two from his flask for the wind, under the moon on a star-filled night, Huebner made a promise to himself. In the ravine he'd lost it. He just kept shooting and shooting his gun. He had to try to stay in control of himself. He thought that was very important. He thought you had to make promises to yourself. In times like these, Lord, a man has to do something. Doesn't he? Poor old Bradley was worried Gentle was crazy; Huebner was worried that he wasn't.

Lieutenant Bradley spent most of his last two days in meetings with Crook and the other officers about their impending expedition, as the General himself liked to call it. The Lieutenant had been in contact by telegraph with Colonel Gibbon in Montana, who by rights was still his immediate superior.

All luck. See you there. ———— be with you.

Bradley didn't quite get the last line and he wondered perhaps if the word God or luck had been omitted.

No one seemed all that optimistic about the next campaign. Crook, for his part, was refreshingly frank.

The best advantage we have, he said, looking out a window at a circled moon, is that most of the new soldiers have no idea what they're getting into.

This was in response to another officer's question about any special orders the General might have about dealing with such fresh recruits in an Indian campaign in the middle of winter in unknown territory.

And this time, the General went on, pulling his beard to full length almost to his waist, we'll have MacKenzie and his boys on our side. If we can find them, we'll git em.

When Crook asked MacKenzie for a comment, he just spat and laughed, drinking openly from a flask. He had an odd laugh that started as a squeak and ended with a cough.

Y'all got any questions? Crook asked.

Yes, sir, an officer named Pavia across the room spoke up. He had on spectacles with his hair combed forward.

Ask it then.

I wonder if you agree it might be better to send out more Indians as scouts. Wasn't that what Custer done?

Crook looked at Bradley. Son?

It's true we just have one now, Bradley said. I giss they got a little scarce after the Bighorn. They ain't much for volunteering.

They lost some men out there. Crook smiled. Colonel MacKenzie, what's your idea here?

Dirt finds dirt, MacKenzie said. His eyes darted to the door then he looked blankly at Crook. The General picked up for him.

If we could keep them in uniform that might be best. After the Bighorn, the government is wary. Do I care what the boys back East think, no. Do I have to listen, yes. We'll have to go with what we got for now.

That MacKenzie seems a bit daft, said one of Bradley's former college colleagues, a man named Jorgeson.

I wouldn't speak so loud. He's looking right at you.

Jorgeson jerked his neck back then ran quickly outside.

He all right? Crook barked at Bradley.

Sure, I think he just needed some air, sir.

Everyone broke into general laughter then when they heard Jorgeson coughing up his dinner in the yard just outside the door.

I'd appreciate a clear shot when we git there, sir, MacKenzie said.

No one of y'all should think that old Crazy Horse is gone to come back peaceably now. Let's not kid ourselves with that shit talk, sir. When he says he'd rather die, I'd like to tend to take the man at his word.

MacKenzie just started talking right out of the blue, after the laughter died down. His voice was calm and low, but no one missed a word. It was eerie.

I giss you men come out here for different reasons. Git some of that gold out here. See the world. Find a wife.

The Colonel laughed, but no one else.

Do you have to defend your home from attackers to truly be a man? MacKenzie addressed the room.

No one knew what to make of this. Maybe the Colonel didn't either. He paused a second then his eyes lighted up again.

I've written down to share with y'all some of the writings of our esteemed and recently departed comrade. Then in an aside, I never did much like him myself.

In the words of Gen'l Custer hisself, MacKenzie rambled on:

The Indians' cruel and ferocious nature far exceeds that of any wild beast on the desert. Nature intended him for a savage state; every instinct, every impulse of his soul inclines him to it.

MacKenzie coughed, took a drink. No one spoke or moved.

Education, he went on, strange as it may appear, seems to weaken rather than strengthen his intellect. Volume after volume might be filled in recounting the unprovoked and merciless atrocities committed upon the people of the frontier by their implacable foe, the red man.

MacKenzie took a drink and sat down. Even Crook looked a little rattled. He called for an end to the meeting for the night and dismissed them to their barracks for the night.

Bradley was standing next to Gentle in the square a few days later where a bunch of MacKenzie's regiment were holding court.

They look more like convicts than soldiers, don't they?

Sir?

C'mon, Private, look at them. They look like a bunch of starved dogs.

I believe half of them come from my home state, sir.

Excuse me, Private Gentle, I didn't . . .

Forgit it. I know it, what you're saying. Where you from, sir?

Richmond, Virginia.

Them's different worlds, there. Anyway I hear them MacKenzies are good at what they do.

Gentle spoke of them as if they all belonged to one family, and with a familial pride.

That they are, Bradley said.

Gentle had found some boys from his home county in the MacKenzie contingent. He spent the last week trying to make friends. They were impressed with his shooting, as anyone would be, but probably because of his age, his fawning and false bragging they treated him much as an errand boy. They didn't like it much the way Bradley and the other officers looked after him either. One day he flat-out challenged a few of them to a fistfight after some stupid, half-imagined confrontation. Neither Huebner nor Bradley were there and both heard about it later at mess, Bradley from one of his fellow officers.

It was bullshit. That boy's plain crazy. They could have killed him just like that. Bam, he's dead.

Bradley shook his head. I hear they went and stuck his head in the latrine, sent him after a flask someone'd dropped.

He'll come to a bad end, that boy. He's with you, ain't he?

Yeah, Bradley spoke up for him, he's a good soldier.

All due respect, Lieutenant, I'd watch that un close.

I intend to.

Time passed. When Bradley finished checking his pack, he decided to make one last round of the camp. Gentle saw him and called
him down. He was sitting under a tree with some boys.

Hey, Cap'n.

Yes, Private Gentle.

That there Indian that ol' Gus been talking to. We going to ride
with him?

You mean the Crow?

Gentle weaved and stumbled a bit, looking for the tree to lean on
and misjudging the distance. Some laughter and catcalls came from
the dark crowd around the tree.

Now, Cap'n.

Private.

Cap'n, I'm here to say I ain't going out with no Indian when we go.

Private Gentle, have you been drinking?

I have, yessir. But I don't see as how that matters t'all to what I'm
saying.

Maybe he wants a sip is all . . . someone called out merrily.

Shit, I'm sorry, Cap'n, here.

Bradley took a quick sip before he spoke.

Hmm, I guess you're right. Bradley scratched his head. Lemme
get this straight then. You're saying you don't want to ride out with us
tomorrow.

This occasioned more laughter and hoots at Gentle's expense.

Cap'n, Cap'n, now hold on. I didn't say that at all.

I didn't think so.

Now looky here, Cap'n, another man spoke up from the darkness. You seem like a smart one.

And a plain-talker, by God, another spoke up.

Yes, sir, continued the first. I wonder could you answer us plain soldiers a question?

I can try, Sergeant.

When are we goin to git our'n?

Excuse me?

Well, now we give the Indians all that land. Signed papers and all. Now come tell, we want it back. Ain't cos it's pretty I don't believe. Damn iffin we're not the ones out here sufferin like dogs. Man's got to wonder what fer. Some say gold, some say God and country. What you say?

Yeah, yeah, what about that? others chimed in.

You think a lot of me, Sergeant. I ain't paid enough to know all that. When they tell me though, I'll let you fellas know.

Some of the men laughed, but not all of them.

You do that, Cap'n, the Sergeant said.

Well, Private Gentle, if that's all, we'll be leaving at dawn with or without you. Maybe you should get some sleep.

With or without me, y' say. Now, Cap'n, I said my piece. That's all.

I understand, Private.

You don't have to go and run me down like that.

You wouldn't want me not to give what I git, would ya? What kind of an officer would I be to you then? Then, turning, Hey here comes Huebner. Why don't you ask him?

Goodnight then, Cap'n, I'll do that.

Bradley nodded once more to the crowd assembled under the tree, and with a wink to Huebner he was gone into the night.

Y'all sure got ya a officer, don't ya, someone spoke up.

Don't you forgit it, Gentle said. Then to Huebner. Hey now, want some whiskey there, German man?

Gentle held up a bottle, empty except for a few drops at the bottom.

Huebner, always polite, took it anyway. He turned it up and drained it down, coughing a bit at the end. What was there was raw and strong, tasting of corn and sandy somehow.

Hey, Gentle whispered. Why'on we git on. I got something's I want to show you. All right, boys, got work to do. We'll see ya in Indian country.

As they walked on, Huebner pitched the bottle into the grass.

Didn't see fit to leave me any, Gentle leered.

He'd taken off his hat, and with his hair sheared close to his skull due to an outbreak of mites and head-lice in the camp he looked like a mouse caught out under the full moon.

Thas a'right, he said.

He produced another full bottle from the recesses of his blue coat.

We ain't empty, Gentle giggled. Sit down now. I got something I want to talk to ya about.

Huebner pulled out two pipes, filled them and handed one over. He lit them in turn and both of them took deep breaths. Both were bundled up, in scarves, extra leggings and coats, but out of the wind the night was clear, now being a nice quiet time to be out in the yard. Neither of them would have been sleeping anyway, waiting for tomorrow.

You really think there's gold out here, Gus?

There's a lot of folks out looking for it anyway. That says something. What you think?

Different things . . . Gentle said and took a drink. Hey, Gus, ya ever do something and then not remember it t'all?

Gentle blew out smoke, looking straight ahead.

You mean drunk?

Huebner nodded at the bottle.

No, not that way. You remember when I shot them Indy-ans?

Yeah, Billy, course I do.

That's the way, Gentle said.

He took a deep breath and as he did, Huebner smelled alcohol and tobacco, homey smells to him.

I don't even remember it m'self, Gentle said.

Speak your mind.

I'm trying ta. I know I done it. I ain't trying to git out of it.

You were excited. You acted on instinct. Everyone does this.

In-stink? What's that? You saying I smell?

Naw, not like that. Like an animal. Like your inside smelled something and you reacted.

What kind of am-inals you mean, German man?

Any one . . .

I'll take a horse, or a wolf, not no chicken or nothing.

That's a bird.

Oh right. I knew that. I remember them riding up . . . Did Bradley shout something?

Mebbe. It all happened at once, Huebner said.

Lieutenant Bradley whut-int too happy when I shot them.

What's the use going through all that agin, Billy?

You know as well as I do. I'm just trying to hold on here.

That ain't in the manual, Huebner said and shook his head.

You said it, German man. Old Gus. Here have one on me, buddy. Yore a'right. You ain't a never been to Tennessee have ya?

Huebner shook his head. It ain't bad here, but it ain't home.

It ain't our'n. That's the land of God there. It ain't like we thought it would be. Back home. Gospel truth.

Huebner nodded. I know it, he said.

I ain't a scared a no Indy-ans. I ain't a scared a no ghosts neither.

Have you been dreaming?

That's when I see it. And I hear them songs they sung that night. It's like I know all the words.

Gentle took back the bottle and took a drink himself.

You ain't never killed nobody before now, have ya? he asked.

No.

It ain't what ya think.

Gentle passed the bottle.

I ain't shamed a what I done.

Gentle looked off, wrapping his arms around his chest and crouching into a ball.

Yeah I never thought, Huebner said. There was a few in the ravine we got.

They were shooting at us.

Hell, we had em pinned down. They didn't have a chance.

We couldn't see.

What?

That's what gits me. Now that ya mention it. We couldn't see em. We could have killed children.

Yeah, we could a.

They were silent. Huebner, after a moment, refilled the pipes.

What about this Indy-an? Gentle asked.

Which one is that?

The one you bin talking to. Do ya think he's all right?

I giss.

Cos' iffin ya do, I'll take your word.

We ain't got much say.

If we did?

He's an Indian. We can trust that, if that's what you mean.

I thought we were fightin agin the Indians.

I giss, like the man done said. There's Indians and there's Indians.

And then there's fools like us. He's just different than us is all, I giss, Gentle mused.

He cocked his head, taking back the flask and another smoke.

Why's he paint his face like that?

Luck, maybe. Religion . . .

You don't know?

I'm not sure I understood it all. We talk mostly with our hands.

He looks like a snake.

He's a Crow, I b'lieve.

Oh, that's what it looks like. Damn bird religion . . .

Gentle laughed and Huebner joined him. It didn't matter how loud they were, with the wind kicking up again. No one could hear them.

He come from Custer, didn't he?

Yep.

You think he's lying?

Nope.

Why ain't he dead? Did he run?

Huebner told Gentle the story the Crow had told him.

That's awful unpolite of the Gen'l.

Gentle shook his head, shivered, said brrr . . .

I told Bradley I wouldn't ride with no Indy-an. Told em that right out.

Is that right?

Ahh, I jes wanted to pick at him a little. He's so serious all the time.

You were joking.

Yeah, half and half. He din't git it though. He thinks I'm an idjit.

What?

Gentle bugged out his eyes and rolled his tongue.

Stupid, he said. Crazed as a starved coon.

They both laughed.

He sticks up for you, Huebner said.

I know it. But he ain't got to act like he has to protect me. I know he thinks that.

It's an officer's job.

He ain't the same with you.

I'm older than he is. He's smart.

Don't git me wrong. Where he goes, so am I.

I could talk to him.

Oh hell no, Gentle said, and shot him a look. It don't matter. Nothing matters out here.

I'll drink to that.

And they did. They smoked again, finished the bottle, and when they finally fell asleep, for a couple hours before dawn, it was right where they sat, mouths fallen wide, warm in their blue coats, not bothering to even get up and go to their barracks.

6

They set out at dawn, Lieutenant James H. Bradley, newly made field Corporals August W. Huebner and William E. Gentle, with their Indian guide Comes Up Red. The Crow took the lead as they rode over old buffalo trails through a winding, green forested creek cut valley. The Crow knew the country and had a good idea where to find the Cheyenne and Sioux they were after.

Sometimes the others mistook the Indian's signal for the bird from which his tribe took its name. They did not always ride together as they had before. The Crow hadn't said anything, but Bradley saw something in his face.

What? he asked. Just say it.

The Crow made signs and with Huebner's help, Bradley got the gist.

He thinks we should split up, Gentle said. He thinks we'll be sitting ducks all out like we are.

All right men, let's spread out. I think we can all take care of ourselves.

They set out along the Powder River. The winter water ran low, clear and blue, cut through the high plains grasslands, into the pine forest mountains. The dirt rode hard and packed. The trees were evergreens grouped in clumps near the water and everywhere else the scrub brush, flowered weeds, long grass and sagebrush were shades of gray brown to darker to almost black brown.

By the afternoon of the first day the snow started to fall. It was as if it had been waiting for them to get away from the shelter of the camp and out into the open. Great, floating flakes they caught in their mouths and let melt softly on their tongues. The snow stayed this way as long as they rode and also when they camped. They tied a blanket to two trees, then set down their provisions, packs and supplies under the shelter it gave. As the night darkened, the intensity of the snow increased steadily and by the hour, until by the next dawn all of them, Comes Up Red included, had come to seek shelter from the storm in the vicinity of the tent. By morning the snow was at least a foot deep. At one point Bradley's horse stopped under a tall pine and would not go on. Red-faced, he had to get down and yank her along by hand until they stopped for the night.

For the next week the squalling blizzard would only let up occasionally and then for at most an hour or two. Through it all they rode on. Once they came off the badland flats into the mountains and forest, the going was slow and they faced some of the toughest country they had encountered in the campaign.

If Crazy Horse took his people here to hide then he picked a pretty good place, Gentle commented one night by the fire, trying to tear off a bite of jerky with his teeth.

They are just trying to survive, Bradley said.

They needn't bother.

On the fourth day of the season of great snows, after they trekked past many bends in the river, through many rises in the great rockface hills Comes Up Red noticed the first signs of the Indian encampment. They had stopped for the night in a clearing on a rise beneath a great rock ledge. They were setting out again in the morning with no letup in the snow when he saw it: a snapped pine twig, snow fallen from the lower branches of the tree, iced over into crystals. He touched the branch and smelled like a dog.

They are near, he said to Lieutenant Bradley.

How can you tell?

The Indian returned the Lieutenant's imploring look with a nod ahead. Bradley whispered something in the Indian's ear and left him to look around once more. Then he called over Huebner and Gentle.

All right, boys.

Yes, sir.

They're out here all right.

I giss we ain't gonna wait for this snow to let up none.

Bradley ignored Gentle's talk and turned to Huebner.

It's important that we do all this in order. Corporal Huebner, you first. I want you to ride out immediately and report back to command. You will tell them where we are and what we've found. Take rations for a couple days' ride and follow the river. It is my understanding that the army should not be more than two or three days' ride behind us.

If I ride straight through, I should get there by tomorrow night.

Exactly.

Bradley paused, blowing on a twig and peeling its bark bare. Huebner nodded and waited for the Lieutenant to finish.

Report directly to Crook if you can, or his Cap'n, John Bourne. I'd rather not go through MacKenzie.

You're saying I should . . .

I'm saying you should go straight to the top—is what I'm saying.

Hopefully we'll be able to give them a chance to surrender first before . . . before—well hell you better git going.

Huebner walked his horse for the first little while. The others watched him mount and disappear into the swirling snow. Bradley next took the shoulder of Corporal Gentle. He stood before him, a half-foot taller, and looked down trying to find his eyes.

Now, we're going to try to talk with them first. When we go, I want to bring you with me.

Why uh—all right. Gentle laughed and reddened.

Don't get me wrong, if they want a fight, we'll surely give them one.

Sir?

No questions now. Here it is, if you so much as make a move for that gun of yours, I'll personally shoot your goddamned hand off.

Sir?

Do you understand me?

Sure I do.

I'm asking for your help.

Sir . . . I—

Gentle, save it. We got some riding to do.

The Crow Comes Up Red waited, already on his red speckled pony. As they rode on up the steep, winding hillside, the Crow told Bradley how many there were, and when they'd last stopped, for how long and for what purpose. The storm did not abate. In the dark forest the difference between day and night was small. Through two more dawns they followed, keeping enough distance as to be undetected.

For the first day after talking to Bradley, Gentle was like a dog shut out of the house. Sullen and quiet, he deferred completely to the directions of their guide. He had trouble with his boots, but he did not complain until on the third night he came back from a walk in the woods by himself with blood on his face and on his shirt.

When Bradley asked him about it, Gentle just wiped it off.

What cha talking about? he said.

They watched another snowy, bruised black and blue sky turn into dark night.

Private, he said. Are you all right?

Jes fine, sir.

But you're shivering. You don't look right.

Well hell, sir, it's cold. Be nice if we could have a fir' jes once through the night.

Bradley looked at the Crow. He built a fire in the hollow of an old dead tree. The Indian motioned for Gentle's boots. The desperate Corporal took them off, placing his blued feet on some stones the Indian had just taken from the fire. The Crow took a number of leaves from the fire and made a bed of them in each of Gentle's boots. With this he handed them back to Gentle, who watched it all wide-eyed, with his feet literally steaming on the rocks.

Well all right, he said through chattering teeth.

Maybe you should try the boots on, Bradley said, suppressing a laugh.

Mebbe I will.

Comes Up Red went off by himself too, for a couple of hours. When he walked back into their measly camp through the driving snow, he reported that they should make camp where they were to wait for the rest of the army. The Indian encampment lay in a valley, a half-day's ride off on the other side of a couple of rises.

You don't think they'll be moving off? Bradley said and waved his arm.

The Indian shook his head.

Under a hole in the trees they made what camp they could and hunkered down to wait for what would happen next.

They're making it easier for us, Gentle said. They're coming back east.

You're turning into quite the good soldier, Corporal.

Thanks, whether you meant it or not. Well now, Cap'n, I wonder how old Gus is doing.

He'll be alright.

Huebner made it back to the army after an exhausting ride down the mountain. He was able to track along the river. Dismounting from his horse in sight of the cook-fire winking red through the black trees, he stumbled over one of the Colonel's men. They sat in a circle under the dark, moonless sky passing around a flask. They offered him a drink and quickly hollered down MacKenzie.

Ahh Bradley's lad, the Colonel said. Welcome, welcome. Did someone give this man a drink?

Sure we did . . .

Well hell, then give him another. Here, sit down, lad. You must have something to tell us. The Colonel kept winking at Huebner as he spoke, emphasizing what seemed like every other syllable with a spit of greasy black tobacco juice onto the snow.

Uh, thanky, sir.

Y'all must have found something out there. Good work, lad. The Colonel's black eyes positively gleamed with the red of the fire dancing before them and heating all their color to an exalted pitch. In the cold he was sweating, with his shirt half open to his waist, exposing a hairy chest pockmarked by a series of deep angry brown scars.

I was instructed to address my report directly to the Gen'l.

In reply to this MacKenzie spat, barely missing Huebner's boots, his face darkened with a spasm of anger and he trembled.

You are a cool one ain't ya. He sent another spray of spit right into the startled Corporal's face. Well Goddamn then, we'll jes have to escort you right there to him now won't we, boys.

They found the General in his tent, set up before his field desk with Captain Bourne nearby, sipping from tin cups before a crackling fire.

Tell me—you've found them—son.

I b'lieve we have, General.

How many days?

Took me one full day to get here.

You rode through day and night?

Yes, sir.

MacKenzie, I take it we can leave in the morning?

That is unless you'd rather get out tonight, sir. The Colonel growled and took a swig from a tin cup offered to him by Bourne, fortifying it with a splash from his flask.

I'm sending you and your boys in first, MacKenzie, he said and looked at Huebner. Excuse me, son. The older man sighed, patiently blowing on a cup of strong-smelling mint tea. Was there more?

Lieutenant Bradley told me to tell you he din't think it was a war party, that well . . .

Is it Crazy Horse?

We don't think so.

Who then?

Cheyenne.

Crook smiled and held out his hand.

Son, I know and respect greatly the work of your Lieutenant Bradley, as does the Colonel, but as far as we're concerned now, they're all war parties. You're welcome to ride back ahead and let the Lieutenant know how we aim to proceed.

I would like to do that, sir.

And, lad, MacKenzie growled. Would you mind thanking him for me too? We'll come and find ya boy when we come after em, the Colonel said. Then we'll all have some fun together.

Huebner got a hot meal, watered and fed his horse with some heated oats from the quartermaster. He had a few drinks with the boys then rode back again through that next night.

Crook's thousand regulars rode toward the village south through the mountains. They marched along the banks of the Powder River, no fires, tough as hide salt beef and hardtack. The army marched over red clay and limestone, straight up for miles, over a ridge and down again. They hiked the narrow mountain passes with picks and shovels, one at a time. They watched the North Star, and kept a steady course to the southwest. Horses gave out, soldiers fell asleep in their saddles and woke up eating dirt. They marched on, through the Valley of the Crazy Woman along the eastern base of the Little Bighorn Mountains, through fierce snowy winds.

After three days and nights they arrived at the site of the Cheyenne encampment. General Crook put MacKenzie in charge. It was very cold, the snow knee deep under the pines and crusted over with ice out in the open. There were over a hundred lodges in a dense stand of willows by the river. The canyon rim surrounded the clearing on three sides, its walls gradating down in shades of brown, red to pale sand. It was a beautiful setting. Command decided to set up through the cold of night and attack at first sign of dawn.

Bradley waited two days for Huebner's return. But instead there was Crook and MacKenzie arriving in the middle of the night with the army. He walked them to the edge of a pine ridge that looked down a long draw to the Indian encampment. A detachment of six soldiers brought out one of the Gatling guns. It was set on a wooden wheel like a cannon. A bank of ten revolving barrels protruded from a wide circular steel shaft. There was a crank in the back and the bullets were dumped into a hopper which fed the head.

I think we should go down in the morning, Bradley said, looking over the gun.

That's the plan, son.

They're sure to surrender.

Crook winked and laughed.

When Bradley looked at MacKenzie, the Colonel just turned and spat a black shoot of tobacco into the snow.

That's a good un, son, Crook said.

The General patted Bradley on the back. The two other officers were still laughing when they left the Lieutenant standing, red-faced and alone, watching the quiet, dark gathering of teepees below. After a while he kneeled down, made a snowball and threw it at one of the trees.

When the dawn was still purple over the gray morning clouds, the soldiers wheeled the Gatling guns to two bluffs, over opposite edges of the colorful canyon walls. The soldiers waved their dirty hankies for ready, and MacKenzie lit his cigar to signal, fire. The round faces of the guns spat bullets at the Cheyenne teepees.

Mercenaries from the Pawnee tribe rode in, while soldiers reloaded, when the smoke from the first barrage still wafted through the winter-crisp first light, cutting down the waking Cheyenne with their stone war-clubs. The Pawnees had slathered their horses with blue paint. Women and children ran out naked into the freezing cold, while the warriors tried to fight with knives, rocks, sticks, with whatever they could grab. The soldiers rode in on their horses and clubbed, then shot, slashed and pummeled them where they stood, man, woman and child.

Lieutenant Bradley stood with other officers some feet from the northside Gatling. He saw old people naked, kneeling over the young to protect them from death that came anyway. Soldiers scalped them, knocked their brains to the snow; MacKenzie's men brandished their knives, ripped open women, clubbed little children; the snowy ground turned muddy red. The mechanical roar of the Gatling guns drowned out everything, even the screams and life-gone cries of the Indians. The bodies of the dead lay steaming, melting the snowy earth, and then freezing as they died in grotesque parodies of supplication, struggle, shock and defiance.

The Lieutenant's eyes kept locking on MacKenzie, out in the middle of the melee, directing his men. Blood dripped from his mouth as if he had kneeled down to drink from the wounds of the dead and dying. The Colonel did kneel; he tried to revive his First Sergeant, McKinney, who had fallen from wounds to the neck and face. When MacKenzie rose, he stood over the fallen Sergeant weeping, as he gave commands to his men to fight on, always through everything.

After a while, Crook dispatched Bradley to mark the trails of the few that got away. At some point he looked back down to the swirling valley of fury and saw Gentle running. Bradley saw him leap in the air. Gentle landed, slipping in bloody snow, between one of MacKenzie's men and the Crow Indian Comes Up Red. The soldier's gun went off. As the smoke cleared Gentle was still shouting into the face of the dazed bluecoat, as if by the fury of his anger he could break the spell of death. Bradley couldn't hear the words from where he stood but his lips read no,

No,

NO.

As the soldier took down his gun, the bayonet tore a hole in Gentle's coat. He shook his head at Gentle, gesturing at Comes Up Red. The Crow stood there still, his own gun drawn, knife between his teeth. Gentle and the soldier faced off, fellow named McGuinn that would die later in the day. For a long second everything stopped. Gentle had turned his head at the last possible instant; the bullet took off a piece of his ear. He rubbed the blood on his face, walking off through the killing field to lean against a tree, checking himself, surprised to still be alive.

Bradley began walking sideways down the trail made by the charge of the soldiers' horses. He lost all track of time. He watched a Cheyenne brave running straight into the line of the Gatling gun. He saw Huebner up there taking a turn on the gun, hitting this one maybe seven times, a distinct checker-square of holes in his chest before the blood showed. The Indian went down and then he got up to his knees. When he fell, Bradley walked by him toward the fray.

By midafternoon MacKenzie's troops had taken torches to all the teepees and burned them down. Thousands of rounds of bullets, hoarded by the Indians and abandoned during the raid, exploded. In the wreckage of the Indian camp soldiers found a pillowcase made from a Seventh Cavalry guidon flag, command memo books and guard rosters; scalps of a white girl and a Shosone girl, a necklace made of human fingers, personal clothing and military hardware.

Anything that didn't look quite dead yet was shot again. Soldiers dragged babbling, wailing squaws out of their tents, held them down for each other inches from their newly dead young. Blood dripped even from the branches of the trees that had been shredded, split and stripped of bark by stray bullets. The fury of the killing seemed to stop even the fall of the snow.

When there were no Indians left to kill, MacKenzie gave the order for the ponies of the village to be lined up against the wall-face of the canyon. When the Colonel gave a holler to Huebner, he turned the crank. The guns shot hundreds of rounds per minute; he kept trying to remember the exact number that people said as he cut through the horses with hail after hail of bullets. It must have only taken maybe a minute to kill them all. Someone had to shake Huebner to get him to stop. He was shooting only stone by then, with shards of rock splintering off and raising a great hail of red clay dust over the fallen bodies of the ponies. When the gunfire ceased finally there were five minutes of what could be called silence, where the dying horses lay writhing.

MacKenzie stood off to the side, dazed, distracted, eyes still fired, sucking on a wound to his arm. The heaving warrior stood there for a long moment, then dropped to his knees. The snow still fell, steadily. MacKenzie stuck out his tongue, a child in a trance. The wind blew; the world had gone on, and he could never kill everything.

Standing amidst the dead and dying, Bradley imagined he could hear MacKenzie breathing. It was like the mouth of the Colonel was right next to his ear.

The Lieutenant would remember that as the moment where everything turned.

Some people lose their minds gradually, unaware. Others watch them go, like a lover, after she has turned and gone. They feel like a slap in the face this new distance between themselves and the world.

This was the way it was for Lieutenant James H. Bradley.

He knew it had happened, and when. The breathing of MacKenzie, hearing it from at least fifty yards away, was the first sign.

The earth is thirsty today, son.

He turned around quickly to see Crook behind him, and together they watched a soldier drag away a woman with a wound to her belly.

You've done good work today, son. You and your men made this great victory possible.

I haven't killed anyone yet.

You should be proud. Your father would be . . . what did you say?

I haven't killed anyone yet. In all this time I haven't. I didn't know it would be like this.

He weaved forward and had to catch himself from falling right out at the General's feet.

Are you all right, son? You been celebrating have ya?

Crook was perfectly magnanimous, clapping a hand on his subordinate's shoulder. One never knows how combat will be, he said, and took a draw from his cigar, looking it over and twirling it slowly with his thumb and forefinger. It is something that cannot be anticipated.

It's a slaughter.

A great victory. That's right, son.

The children, the women . . . Bradley went on again, almost falling over, looking for a place to lean he grabbed the General's shoulder.

Crook was a little startled. Maybe you need to go ahead and sit down. We can fight ourselves too hard. Have you checked on your boy? Wasn't he hit before?

Uh—n-no. I-I-I haven't.

You haven't been drinking? Maybe you should sit down, son. Have you checked on Gentle?

What?

I believe one of your scouts was shot. You must be concerned. Don't let me keep you.

Bradley tried a salute, stumbled one more time badly, as he tried to walk up the hill. Crook watched, shaking his head, making a note to see if he were ready for duty tomorrow. It would be hard to replace him.

Near dusk, the Cheyenne Chief Dull Knife shouted down from the rim of the canyon. He'd lost three sons, one of the uniformed interpreters said. He said he was ready to surrender.

MacKenzie said he was ready too. He was distraught over the losses of his men. Let the goddamned Cheyenne take care of themselves, he told Crook.

This was the last thing Bradley heard before he passed out.

When Bradley awoke, Corporal Gentle and Comes Up Red hovered over him, wiping what tasted like blood and vomit from his mouth with a cold, wet rag. Gentle and Comes Up Red came back to the scout camp after saving the day for McKinney's troops, slathered in blood, reeking of their kills. Bradley spoke up first.

You all right, Gentle?

Ahh shit, just a scratch, sir. Under his hat a raggedy bandage, blood reddened, was wrapped all around one side of his head from ear to crown.

Bradley moved to rise, but he could not.

Maybe you should just sit right there, Cap'n.

Is everything over with?

I think old MacKenzie and his boys have got everything pretty well in hand. It'll be dark in a few minutes. We can just as well make us a fire right here.

Comes Up Red had already in fact started gathering wood and set to this purpose. Bradley spat in the snow. His mouth tasted like steel.

Water? he said. William Gentle, do you have some water?

You ain't hurt anywhere you ain't telling us about, now is ya, Cap'n?

I am perfectly fine, Corporal Gentle. I just can't seem to get up.

That's all right then. We need to set a spell anyways.

Gentle held one of his arms close to his chest as if it were in a sling. With the other he unhitched his canteen from his belt and handed it to the Lieutenant. He had to hold it for him.

You sure you ain't hurt nowheres, sir?

You are the wounded one, Bradley said, wiping his mouth between thirsty gulps. I'm fine.

Comes Up Red had come back with wood and now leaned over a branch, blowing on it lightly until a flame held and he could add more fuel. They sat back to watch.

As night fell, all of them got drunk.

After the horses, Huebner had gone off by himself. He rejoined them after a long walk alone in the woods.

Gentle kidded him about the horses. Horse killer, he'd say and giggle.

When they laughed, Bradley, Comes Up Red and then even Huebner joined in. What else could he do?

I giss we killed them all, Huebner said. He sat down and drank from the bottle.

Not all, Bradley slurred out. We h-have ta foller the blood on the snow. That's what we have to do. They left a trail.

What is he talking about? Huebner asked Gentle, as if Bradley were not there.

It's all right. He's a little crazy from something. He'll be all right. He's better now.

Gentle showed them a string of scalps. The Indian-man showed me how to scalp someone, he said.

You saved him. Bradley said. I saw it.

You're durn right I saved his red-ass Injun life, Gentle said, and slapped the Crow on the back. Looky here, Cap'n.

When Gentle held up the string of scalps in his face, Bradley threw up again.

We have to follow the blood, he said, and wiped his mouth with his coat sleeve.

Whatever is he going on about?

I think we orter let it go for now. He's been a real good Cap'n up to now.

A wounded soldier approached out of the darkness. Ken a man join y'all? he asked.

Give that man a blanket, Bradley says. That man is shivering.

No one moved.

I am an officer of the United States Army—you must follow an order given by a superior. He turned to Gentle. Corporal, who is that man?

Why that's Tom Salley, from MacKenzie's boys.

That man is dying. Give him a blanket. We can't save him, but we can make him feel better.

No one moved, then finally Comes Up Red offered his blanket to the man, who took it and sat down, mumbling something to himself.

What is he saying?

No one answered. No one could tell. Bradley drifted off to something somewhere else. They all did.

The man called Salley was dying. He had an arrow in his back. At one point someone noticed that he had stopped mumbling. They were all piss drunk by then. They faded in and out of something like sleep, waiting for the dawn, waiting for the order to come so they could leave all this behind. Suddenly he was dead among them.

That guy, Bradley said, he's not shivering anymore. Gentle, check on your friend.

The snow fell through the night, turning them into white mounds.

We're all the same, Bradley was talking again. I'm just like MacKenzie . . .

Cap'n, Gentle said, begging your pardon, sir, but what in the hell are you talking about?

Huebner tapped Gentle's shoulder and put a finger to his lips.

But he's talking crazy.

The Crow Indian Comes Up Red passed the bottle to Gentle.

As a scout, Bradley went on, as a guide, I thought I was different. I had a skill.

You do, Cap'n, Gentle said. You got us here.

Right, I'm a bloodhound, a sniffing dog. He made snuffling sounds.

Cap'n, can I get ya some water? Huebner offered.

Naw, but I'll take some more of that whiskey y'all are passing around.

Cap'n, are you sure you ain't been hit?

It's all right, Gentle. I'm raving. We are hoping it will pass. I know it, but I can't help it.

Sir? Are you cold? Can you sleep, sir?

Gentle, I'm going to die out here.

Where are you hit, Cap'n? Just tell me where you're hit.

The Indian made a motion with his hands, like an explosion, tapping his head.

Right, that's it, Cap'n, you just got a shock, t'day. Hell, all of us did.

Gentle, you got shot . . .

That's right, Cap'n. Gentle touched his bandage. So why don't you snap the hell out of it. You're scaring me.

I didn't get shot. I got shock.

There ya go! That's it.

Huebner took the bottle from Bradley. Did you check on your friend? he asked Gentle. That man over there from Tennessee?

I did.

And he's all right?

He's asleep.

I'm not so sure, Corporal. Bradley tried to get up to look for himself, but his legs wouldn't work. No, he said, waving his arms. Something is wrong with that man.

Gentle waved him off. Here, he said, I'll go and check him agin. Goddamn.

What is it, Corporal?

Gentle put his hand on the cold form and said, He's frozen. He's frozen stiff. He's with them Indians now. Cap'n Bradley, he's dead.

I knew it. I knew it.

Goddamn, Cap'n.

What?

What can we do?

There is nothing, Gentle. You can just let him sit there. The snow will cover him up. The snow covers everything up wonderfully. Don't you think so, Huebner?

Huebner nodded. Whatever you say, Cap'n. But he looked really shaken.

I bet Comes Up Red can give us one of those wonderful Indian words for this. Look over there, children dead, mothers raped, all covered now by snow.

Cap'n, I think that'll be enough, Huebner said, and stood up.

You want me to stop, soldier?

I just said I thought that was enough, sir.

What are you going to do? Is that an order? Are you giving an order to me?

Cap'n . . .

Bradley suddenly quieted. He looked sad.

If I could stop it, Gus, don't you think I would? Don't you think?

Goddamn, c'mon y'all quit all that. This man is dead. We let him die right out in front of us.

That's wrong, Gentle. We didn't kill him. He would have died anyway. You have to believe that. Bradley's trance-like manner unnerved Gentle more. He yanked on Salley's arm.

We orter do something. He's from Tennessee. C'mon y'all.

People die from Tennessee too, Corporal Gentle.

We should do something for him. Goddamn y'all. C'mon, Gus. Indian man. Gimme a hand here. Mebbe we can bury him.

For this, we are thankful for the snow.

Cap'n, Cap'n, stop it, please.

You can pray if you like. You can ask the Indian man and the German man to help you carry him down the hill.

Could we? Do you think we should, sir? Now you're talking some sense . . .

Surely, Corporal Gentle, you can throw him on the pile with the rest of the dead.

Cap'n, stop it.

Or maybe with the horses. A man from Tennessee, maybe he'd like to be with all the ponies.

I say we orter do something. Boys, will ya help or not?

The ground is frozen solid, Corporal. No one will be buried today. There is nothing to be done. There is nothing we can do for the dead.

Sir?

What is it, Huebner?

What about us?

Huebner, is that you? I'm having trouble with my eyes.

Yes, sir. What are you saying? What does that make us? I killed those horses. I was on that big gun half the day, women and children. Are you saying we can't hope for . . . ?

Absolution, pardon, freedom from guilt?

Bradley closed his eyes, like he was trying to remember something, to concentrate. He sighed deeply.

There is nothing we can do. There is nothing.

Stop it. Stop talking like that sir, Gentle said, and looked at Huebner, who took Bradley by the arm.

Cap'n, maybe you should rest, he said.

Damnit, I'm going to have to ask all of you to stop talking to me at once. I am raving. I am not myself. Stop talking like what, Gentle? What is *what?*

Ahh, sir, please say some o' that manual talk you usually use. Maybe I liked you better when you didn't tell . . .

Tell what? Tell the truth? No Gentle, this is OK. I will be OK, and so will you.

And tomorrow we ride, the Crow spoke up.

Yes, exactly. See the Indian understands.

Mebbe you're right, Huebner said. I know you're a little crazy right now. And all of us have been drinking.

That's it, Corporal. I am crazy and I'm right.

I jes wish there was something we could do for old Salley, Gentle said, downcast.

He has his blanket. We can go to sleep. As the Indian says, to-morrow we ride. If you want though, I will pray with you.

Ahh hell, Cap'n, I don't know any prayers. I know the Our Father . . . I allays jes mumbled the rest. Besides sir, I smell like I killed the whole tribe. And we been drinking. The Indian here, pardon me feller, he ain't even no Christian, sir.

It's all right. I know it. Just say the prayer after me.

They joined hands then, all of them, and they prayed. It did not change anything. It did make them feel a little better. They were able to be quiet for the rest of the night. Huebner had some tobacco. He filled pipes and passed them around. They finished the bottle. They could do nothing more for the man from Tennessee.

7

When Bradley awoke the next morning, he was alone. The snow was still there, but he could not make anything else out. Bradley was having trouble with his eyes. He was having trouble keeping the sequence of events straight in his mind. When everything cleared, he saw they were on a bluff, a ledge cut into the rock-face of the valley. Gentle and Comes Up Red had gone to tend to the horses, Huebner to report to command. It was just him and the dead man from Tennessee, stiffened up some since the night before. He couldn't be sure if he'd given orders and dispatched the three other scouts or they volunteered on their own. They were good soldiers. They knew what to do. It didn't matter really one way or the other. It mattered that he wasn't sure.

He was having trouble with his eyes. There were flashes, and stretches very blurry like snow falling. Gentle was the first to notice. Bradley found them watering the horses by a spring that trickled down the stone face of the canyon, turning the mineral rock a red rusted color where it ran down the side.

Cap'n, what are you looking at?

Nothing . . .

Sir?

Gentle stood beside him, and held his arm steady. Had he slipped? Bradley couldn't remember. Lieutenant Bradley knew he made it down the wet slope, grabbing here on a clump of withered weeds, there on a rock jutted out from the wall. He remembered these details but not the climb down itself.

I can't see so well right this minute, Corporal Gentle. It comes and goes.

The Lieutenant blinked and his eyes cleared. They stood away from the center of the camp. There was no snow left where the battle had taken place, where MacKenzie had burned the ground. The bodies had been stacked, American on one side, Indians to the other. In a few minutes they would be leaving it all behind.

Cap'n, mebbe you should go for sick call, Gentle said.

No, soldier, I don't b'lieve that would be such a good idea for me.

You said some strange things last night, Cap'n.

We all did. You're the one had his head near blown off. I don't see you in the hospital.

Bradley looked at Comes Up Red, who had cocked his head to listen. Gentle caught the look and followed the Lieutenant's eyes. The Crow nodded his head down, no. Gentle backed off.

Really, Gentle, the Lieutenant said. I'll be all right in a minute. It's just something that comes and goes.

All right.

Anyway, how's your ear?

It hurts like hell, but they been giving me something for it. Makes me dopey.

Morphine.

Shit ain't no good for ya, Cap'n. I jes poured a bunch of alcohol on it.

That's one way to do it.

There ya go, Cap'n. Sounds more like you.

When Huebner met with Crook to report for morning duty, the General asked him pointedly about Bradley

He's already off with the Crow. They're checking on trails.

That boy never does stop, does he? The General shook his head approvingly.

Huebner smiled and nodded. Maybe the old guy knew something, maybe not. Maybe he didn't care.

Well, y'all take care when ya go. Sometimes, son, y'all have to make allowances for each other, he said.

He knew, Huebner realized.

Have you been to see the Colonel, MacKenzie? Crook asked him. He seems kind of fond of you, son. I think he'll be glad to know you come through it all all right yesterday.

No'm. Should I?

Let's go see'm, Crook said.

MacKenzie had not left the field hospital since they'd set it up, at the south end of the camp, where the ground went off straight and level into the deep green woods. He sat on the trunk of a red ash tree. The tree'd been split wide open by gunfire and leaned to the side.

We had four more to die through the night, MacKenzie said.

He didn't seem to recognize Huebner, at first, but all at once something changed in his eyes.

You done right on that gun yisterdee, son.

Huebner swallowed. It was hard to look at MacKenzie.

I hope you see why we got to do this. The Colonel looked around at his men, laid out on cots or on the cold bare earth with just blankets for warmth. MacKenzie had cooked big pots of tea and soup.

He played nursemaid to his wounded men as he called around, checking on their conditions. There was one whose leg they'd taken off who didn't seem to know it was gone.

MacKenzie shook his head.

He keeps trying to get up, the Colonel said. He'll fall all over himself and try again. What are ya gone to tell a feller like that?

Is he going to make it? Crook asked.

Probably not. MacKenzie shook his head again and spat on the ground.

Don't tell him a damn thing then, said Crook. Let em think what he wants.

That's what I say. MacKenzie looked pale and sick. But sometimes my true-heart, it don't agree.

Huebner just looked at him and stayed quiet. He couldn't think of anything to say. He thought of his last moments on the gun the day before, heard again MacKenzie's order to kill. He realized what were horses to him were something else to this man. Something happened; he was sure he didn't know what it was. It could happen to any of them. Given enough time it would happen to all of them. It had already started.

Crook and Huebner left MacKenzie with his men.

Now you see how important y'all are, Crook said. Some of the others said mebbe y'all ain't right for this. That we should send more of our Injuns to scout, but . . .

We ain't ready to quit, Huebner spoke up.

All right now, Crook said, and slapped Huebner's back. We gonna send off these men right, then we're going to send you fellers after them reds. Y'all be ready now.

The snow turned to rain as the day went on. It softened up the ground and they at least were able to bury the bodies. MacKenzie in-

sisted on holding a full-dress funeral before they went anywhere, before they followed the trail of the Indians to find Crazy Horse's
camp. In the afternoon MacKenzie rallied during the funeral procession. They walked down through the woods to the river. He and
Crook each made a speech. A fellow named Sam John Mangus said
the sermon.

I've lost fifteen men, MacKenzie said. Never lost fifteen men before. Never lost even five.

A shaved bald Scot name of Green blew his bugle. They shot off
their guns then everyone stood around for a few minutes looking embarrassed.

Before the four scouts left the camp, Huebner walked over to the
dead horses. In the night they had frozen just like he'd shot them.
Fearful and confused. He couldn't even pray. He stood there for a
long time, moving his lips and listening to the rain pelting the
corpses' hides. He counted 127 dead horses and then walked away
to join the others.

When the Crow, Gentle and Huebner had followed
Bradley to the edge of the camp, Bradley stopped them before they
rode on. There was a small impossibly bright blue waterhole for the
horses. Ahead of them a thicket of leaveless brown willows leaned
into the wind. Everything else wore the same wintry gray to white
pallor. Bradley took it all in with one deep breath then turned back
to his men.

Any one of you can go back with the rest of the troop to the fort,
he said, listening to his words to keep them steady. He looked at each
of the men in turn.

Gentle looked away quickly, checking his rifle.

I giss it's the breeze that keeps this water from icing over, he said.

I'll take that you want to keep on.

No place else to go, Gentle said, watching the swells that licked at the frost-tipped grass by the waterside.

Gus? Bradley looked at the German.

I b'lieve Colonel Gibbon is waiting for us back with our own troop. We don't want to disappoint him.

Bradley wiped his eyes and nodded gratefully. When he finally turned to the Crow, he had already ridden ahead. A bare stone face rose out of the willows beyond the thicket. The Indian walked his horse toward it, his gaze turned toward what daylight was left in the sky.

The scouts found more dead horses on their fourth day out. They were bloated and turning to black. They'd been gutted, with blood and entrails beside in the snow. The scouts came out of the deep pinewoods, carefully guiding their mounts on foot across the sheet of ice that covered their trail since the cold came on again.

The Crow Indian found a baby, stiff and covered with blood, inside one of the horses.

What the hell?

Comes Up Red made motions: the Cheyenne out in the cold, freezing to death.

They must have put the children in there to save their lives, Huebner said.

Comes Up Red took out his blade and took the baby's scalp.

Ahh Hell, Indian man, Gentle squawked. Why'd ya go and do that?

Comes Up Red, Bradley said. If you're, uh, finished I think we should get out of here.

This is awful.

Gentle?

I'm jes tired, Cap'n. Sometimes out here I jes get awful tired.

No one answered.

The others turned to lead their horses away. Comes Up Red lashed the scalp to his string, its fresh blood dripping onto the clear white ice. They stepped gingerly and the horses' hooves crunched. There was no other sound but the wind and then again, Gentle. He stood there alone.

All these dead horses, he said. This ain't no good. This is just bad, y'all.

Huebner went back for him. He took Gentle's horse with his free hand and walked slowly after the others. They gave Gentle all the time he needed to catch up.

They walked in an open field. Cat-tail shoots poked up through the snow. Gentle, when he finally moved on, picked one of the stalks and chewed on it.

The scouts split up from the army. The other troopers had gone on to Fort Keough in the Montana Territory for reinforcements and medical care. The scouts were left to follow the trail of the runaway Cheyenne.

Their horses suffered and so did they. They rode over rocky cuts, dry riverbed cuts, giant rock shelves, desolate and flat, toward distant buttes, red brown on top, with stark drops and folds in the earth, snow-covered long rolling hills and high desert plains. The cold, dry wind cracked their lips and turned their cheeks raw with its icy fire.

They found an old couple died together, naked in the snow. They had wrapped their arms around each other.

Ya think someone took their clothes after they died? Gentle asked.

Naw, I think they must'a gave em away before, Huebner said.

They knew they were gone to die, Bradley said, they gave their clothes away.

Comes Up Red nodded.

Goddamn, said Gentle.

The Crow took the scalp of each of the dead they came upon, young and old alike. Each time, before and after, he kneeled in prayer. No one tried to stop him.

Whenever a Crow meets Sioux or Cheyenne, one has to die,

But they're already dead.

The Crow just looked at him.

Once Bradley asked if they'd all like to join the Crow in prayer.

Yeah, Cap'n, I would, said Gentle.

Why don't you lead us, Corporal?

All right, by God. Let's all take our hats off.

Corporal Gentle led them in the Lord's Prayer. When he was done, he looked at Bradley.

Cap'n, do you think it be all right if I blessed my mama?

Yes, that ought to be fine. I think you can do that for all of us.

They found the evidence of old campfires, the picked clean carcasses of ponies. Whenever they saw blood somewhere on the trail, they knew they were going the right way.

Bradley dreamed of horses, a black sky, black earth, a streak of metallic silver on the horizon like the shiny barrel of a rifle, a black horse against the silver, two white horses facing him, eating. He heard grass pulled from the soft earth. One of the white horses was looking right at him when he awoke. A light came on, bright sunlight dappling green grass, pine seedlings, the shadows of trees. His head exploded with pain, his throat caught. There were many birds, talking to each other, the beating of their wings lifting off the earth through the trees, up into the sky. He awoke smelling wildflowers, but there weren't any around.

They chewed on sticks when they were hungry. They tightened their belts and rode on. Seldom could they mount their horses, they never knew when they might hit a bad patch. They slipped and fell many times. They had ripped pants and bruises all over their knees and shins.

Sometimes it was funny when they fell. Bradley took a great tumble, head over heels down a long winding trail. He lost his grip on his horse and it stood there with the others and watched. He ran straight into a bank of pine straw at the bottom of a stand of old evergreens. They all held their breath until they saw Bradley's face and heard his laughter.

Here, sir, I got yourn horse.

Took a bit of a tumble, Bradley said, when Huebner and the others reached him.

Sure as I'm standing here.

Thanky. He brushed the snow, ice and pine-straw off his clothes. Let's ride on, he said.

Huebner and the Crow Indian Comes Up Red competed to see who could build the biggest bonfires. Once Gentle sighted and shot straight out of the sky a couple of Canadian geese. They led an entire flock and all of them got off a few good shots. They plucked the feathers and roasted the birds on spits over a banked fire of red coals.

Bradley's condition seemed to get a little better each day. He learned a few tricks to help him not to feel. He tried to believe there was nothing he could do to change anything that happened. Whenever they found more dead Cheyenne along the trail, he felt more and more numb. Maybe this would be what would help him to live.

How you doing, Cap'n? Gentle asked him by the fire one night.

The flames cooked their faces red and made their clothes steam rankly with the smell of their bodies when they stood close to it.

I guess like the rest of us I could use a little sunshine, Gentle. Thank you.

Hell, Cap'n, we're all this side of the devil.

Sure.

Can I ask ya something?

Yep.

Do you remember what all you said that night?

Naw, I don't, not everything. I have an idea. It's not all a blank.

All right then, there's something else . . .

Yes, Corporal Gentle?

We're out here chasing around a bunch of starving, dying Indians.

And?

I ain't going to ask you why, but—well—I think I got an idee what you were trying to do back there.

Thank you, Corporal Gentle.

Don't be skeered to call em out.

Corporal?

The devil, God either one . . .

All right, Gentle. I . . .

You should pray more, Cap'n. All of us should pray all the time we can.

You must be right.

Right as rain, Cap'n.

When they saw the first skeleton, they didn't realize where they were. They'd followed the trail of the dying Cheyenne along the river. Snow fell lightly on the water. Where there was no snow there were bare dirt spots, sudden deep gulches, rust-colored mineral rock, exposed folds in the dirt. Under a hazy sky with pale shades of blue. They came out of a black willow thicket, broke off the icy branches when they tried to brush them away. Huebner saw the first one. It looked like a scarecrow. They'd come in on their horses and now Comes Up Red dismounted first. He waded through the knee-deep powder drifts up to the rise. He stood there before two stakes tied with rope like a cross. A Union blue coat, Seventh Cavalry, had been draped over with a skull placed on top.

Step back, Indian man, Gentle said just loud enough for everyone to hear. He unslung his rifle. Without a word Huebner and Bradley joined him and they shot until the blue coat lay on the snow.

You white men do some strange things, the Crow's face said.

They all just stood there, their heavy breath white before their open mouths. None of them looked at any of the others.

That was your own man, the Crow spoke up.

It won't anymore, Gentle said.

Don't ask us to pray now.

I wasn't gonna.

This is where Custer camped the night before the battle, the Crow said.

They put it here for a reason.

They're trying to spook us.

They ain't doing a bad job.

All three looked over at the Crow.

Why didn't you say anything?

He just shrugged his shoulders. He'd taken to wearing his blue coat over his bare torso. He dyed his chest red. A steady snow fell.

They must have dug that up for us to see.

Maybe we didn't bury all the bodies last summer.

Naw, I think we got them all.

Should we be walking around here at all?

This is just one big graveyard.

This field?

The whole damn cun-tree.

They found five more of the scarecrows, one on the hill where Reno made his stand, one down in the death coulee. They found three more of them grouped together on the hill where they'd buried most of the dead. An early crescent moon hung pale over the rolling and twisting country, snow filling the sandy desert bowls one after the other for miles, stark white broken only by the black spines of dead trees.

They spent the day walking around out there. The snow never let up. With the rest they took turns shooting them down. They talked very little. For once the Crow Indian said more than the other three combined, though no one understood a single word. As dusk fell, and the whole world grew toward darkness, Comes Up Red led them to a place downriver to camp for the night. Where the four scouts finally rested they could look over the burial hill, the death coulee, over the rolling cut hills. Though it was mostly dark now, they could see forever.

We ain't alone out here, Gentle said.

No one asked what he meant. They built a modest fire on the banks of the icy river and sat watching the sparks fly and fade into the dark. A low and dense fog line swirled over them off the river. For a time they could not even see each other. They talked through it.

I'd have been satisfied never to come here again, Bradley said.

Boy, I could sure use a drink, Huebner said.

I heard that, Gentle answered.

Wait a minute, Bradley said, fishing in his saddlebag.

I cain't believe it.

Where'd y'all git that, Cap'n?

Gen'l Crook gave it to me. When we were on the hill watching the MacKenzie massacre.

He thought you might need it?

Yeah, I jes stuffed it into my pocket, forgot about it till we got on the trail later.

When the fog cleared, the night stood around them cold and clear. There were no stars. Mindful of the spirits of the unsettled dead, they camped by the river. The water turned black by the night, whispering of time. They got shit-drunk and did imitations of each other. Gentle did Lieutenant Bradley, stutter and all. Bradley surprised them all with a dead-on MacKenzie, Custer quotes included. Huebner and the Crow Indian traded almost-mute mimics of each other.

Do you think those dying Cheyenne did all this?

Must a been . . . who else?

The Crow Indian Comes Up Red shook his head. Crazy Horse, he said.

You think?

The Crow smiled oddly and nodded.

He needs to die, Gentle said.

8

Lieutenant Bradley spent a night at Fort Keough. He left the Crow Indian Comes Up Red in the field with Corporal Gentle and went with Corporal Huebner to meet his former Commander, Colonel Gibbon. Bradley had a splitting headache that made his eyes water. He had to hold his right hand to keep it from shaking. Today was a bad day for him.

The snow was sparse here though it'd been heavy all around the camp. For some reason this small section had been missed by the storms. The fort was set on a stark hilltop overlooking a long grassland valley, high winds, blue sky shrouded by wispy white clouds, distant long and rolling with lush pinelands to the south and wide open aboriginal, volcanic desert-lands. A dry cut creekbed filled with different colored stones and glass fragments glittered by the light of the sun. Bradley sent Huebner to the quartermaster for new outfits for their horses and then joined Gibbon on the porch swing in front of the officer's quarters. Gibbon sipped a glass of whiskey and chewed a cigar. He had a blue and brown patterned Indian blanket wrapped around his shoulders for the cold.

Compliments of the Sioux, he said to Bradley when he looked at the blanket. Want one?

Nah, I'm all right. I will take a drink.

That's the boy, the Colonel said, and coughed. So y'all going out with us this time, the Colonel said.

Guess so, sir, said Bradley. What happened to MacKenzie?

He and Crook were called to Washington.

S'at so?

Yes, sir. Crook's reporting on our great victory over the Cheyenne.

MacKenzie?

Seems like they're a little worried about the inauguration. They elected that new feller with Grant gone. Now they're worried they might have trouble gittin him in.

Grant's gone?

Yeah, some other feller, Hayes or Rutherford, what's his name? Seems like a bunch of soldiers are making noise about taking over the White House.

Really?

A sort of coup d'état.

So they sent in MacKenzie.

You got it, James. They sent over MacKenzie and his boys to make sure everything goes well with the transfer of power.

Divide and conquer.

Something like that, Gibbon said, and took a drink, rinsing his teeth with the liquor before swallowing. He looked at Bradley, then continued.

I take it you boys found what you were looking for out there?

I believe we did.

Tell it.

We followed the runaway Cheyenne all the way out here.

Heard it was Dull Knife and Little Wolf.

Right.

What about Crazy Horse and his band?

It looks like that's where the others were heading for.

Where are they?

He and his band are holed up in the valley out at Box Elder Creek.

You still got the same crew as before?

Yes, sir. We've come through it all right. I left Gentle out there with this Crow guide we picked up in Fort Robinson. Huebner's here with me.

How are y'all holding up? Gibbon asked.

He looked at Bradley's hand and then at the floor when the Lieutenant caught him, kicking some sagebrush off the porch.

We made it here.

How's that Indian working out?

He knows this land. He handled himself pretty well with the Cheyenne.

They don't mix too well do they, Gibbon said, and laughed.

Naw, neither with the Sioux.

Guess not.

They led us right back through Little Bighorn.

Who did?

Dull Knife and Little Wolf, whoever else survived.

That's something. How are things down that way?

Bout the same, Colonel, bout the same.

How bout the other two, Gentle and Huebner? Y'all have spent some time together.

They're both good men, sir.

I hear they got their feet wet with the Cheyenne.

Bradley didn't speak right away. He took a drink and exhaled very slowly.

Now, son, he said, let me say something straight out. General Crook seemed a little worried about you after the Cheyenne battle.

Sir?

Bradley used both hands to finish his drink.

You didn't do anything wrong, son. They just said you had a hard time out there.

With the Cheyenne?

Yes, son. Now if something happened out there. If you need to talk about it, well . . .

Bradley motioned with the glass toward the bottle and the Colonel refilled it for him. The Lieutenant swallowed, licked his lips, watching the flask, his glass and his hands.

I took an oath as an officer of this country's army. I'm here to do whatever my duty entails, sir.

Well said. I just wonder how you and your boys are doing on the entails part, son. My stripes are on the line too.

You want the truth, sir?

What part you think bears tellin. Any good soldier's got some things just betwixt him and the Lord. We can be clear on that. I ain't askin . . .

Naw, I know, Colonel, and I appreciate it. You see, when we went in I understood our orders to be to bring them back if we could. If they would come. I wasn't sure if all those Cheyenne needed to die out there. I'm still not sure.

They would have surrendered? You thought?

I did, sir. A lot was lost on both sides. Colonel MacKenzie took a pretty good beating himself.

Son?

I been thinkin on it, Colonel. I'm a Lieutenant. It ain't my business who lives and who dies.

That's right, son. But there wasn't anything you did? Anything that happened to you?

I didn't do a damn thing.

You think you should have?

I ain't no God, sir.

None of us are out here. We ain't no angels either.

Gibbon looked again to Bradley's hands. Bradley caught his eyes and shrugged.

Lemme tell you something. Maybe you don't know some things about that Bighorn mess. Reno had a man, Charley Reynolds, shot right next to him. Had to leave him there, son. Imagine what that might do to a man.

Sir, I remember how he was that night in the rain at the river.

That weren't the half of it, son. What thanks did he git? They put him on trial, tried to take away his rank.

I heard there'd been an inquiry. I didn't hear the result.

Hell, he's a ruined man, Gibbon said, and looked at the Lieutenant's hands. Mind me, James, the Colonel spoke low and looked off to a place far away in the sky where the sun was out.

Bradley finished his glass.

They got the wrong man, they did.

Sir?

Custer's the one what caused all that mess.

The Colonel took a long drink from the bottle. Your family's given a lot to this man's army, James Bradley. We just want to keep you around. You've got a fine future to look to.

I guess I just seen a lot of things the last year, sir.

I guess you have at that.

Colonel, can I ask you a question?

Shoot.

You going to let me keep going out or what?

Son, I chose you as the chief of scouts.

Gibbon took a long draw from his cigar. He had let it go out and had to light it again before he continued.

Hell, James, if you're ready, it ain't nothing I'm ever going to question.

Thank you, sir.

Hell, don't thank me.

The Colonel spat as far as he could, but didn't clear the bottom step. His wad made a speckled brown indent in the snow.

You think we got a chance at them at this Box Elder Creek?

I believe we do, sir.

That's right down below here, ain't it?

Tough spot, Colonel. I told Gentle and the Crow to take their best shot while we were gone.

Did you now? They going to take on the whole Crazy Horse band?

They would if I let them.

They both laughed.

I told them to keep an eye on them.

They really got their boots to our necks to git this done.

That's what I thought.

Gentle and the Crow camped in a red clay gulley cave in a snowstorm. They rode through lush green piney hills where the snow had frozen on the branches and weighed them down blue. They stalked the woods and the walls of the canyon; the Sioux held their ground.

The army left next morning and rode all day. It was almost dusk when they reached Box Elder Creek. More than fifteen hundred regulars entered the valley in a long winding line in the pass between two tall buttes.

Gentle met Bradley in the pass there shadowed by the northern-side butte.

How's it look, Corporal Gentle? Bradley asked, saluting.

We ready now, sir, Gentle said and nodded toward the Crow, who sat grazing his horse in a patch of tall grass beneath a twisted cottonwood tree.

Where are they? asked Gibbon.

Right up yonder hill. Gentle took off his hat and pointed toward a long snow-covered rise.

Waitaminute son, Gibbon spat out. Whose man is that?

Can't say.

What's he doing up there?

Wait, look, on the hill, there's Indians up there too.

That's why we couldn't git close, Cap'n.

Is he alive Gentle? Bradley asked.

He is wearing a blue coat. He looks like one of our'n. We haven't been able to risk it.

Sioux surrounded the soldier on the hill. Despite the biting cold the braves were stripped to the waist, their chests painted red. A ravine cut into the rise behind, where the ancient glacial earth had folded in upon itself. The wind rushed down the hill and swirled around the soldiers at the bottom. Every time Gentle opened his mouth it burned his lungs.

Do you think we should rush it? Gibbon asked.

That's what we've been waiting on, sir, Gentle said.

All right then, Gibbon said. He motioned over an officer and word was passed. A gray sun had dipped all the way behind the bare rock tip of the butte.

Hell, it's a little late, but we can't leave him there.

At the Colonel's signal the troops kicked their mounts and dashed up the wall of the canyon. They made progress for maybe fifty feet before the snow started to give all at once under the hooves of their horses. When the snow loosened from the pounding of the horses' hooves there was a sheet of ice underneath. The men and horses started to slide on top of one another. There was an avalanche of horses and men.

An ear-piercing scream sounded on the hill and an Oglala brave put a torch to the soldier and set him afire.

Only one man made it to the top. A fellow name of Ames, someone said. He was shot and left for dead at the foot of the burning soldier.

The troopers were in chaos for the next few hours as the sun set red over the darkening high plains. The horses with broken legs had to be shot, the soldiers' wounds attended to in turn.

August Huebner saw the man named Ames fall.

I'm going after him, he said to Bradley.

You're going to what?

Damnit sir, we can't just leave him up there.

At least take someone with you. Where's Gentle?

I don't know, sir.

Is he all right? Where's the Crow?

I don't know, sir.

No one's ordering you to go up there.

I know it.

You're going to go up there anyway, aren't you?

Yes, sir.

Be careful, soldier.

It's getting on dark, sir. Those Indians won't be up there no more.

Well, if you see any, how about leaving em alone. We will need you tomorrow.

Huebner crouched down as he climbed slowly up the icy slope. He put one hand in front of the other, pulling himself up to get a good hold. His firearm strapped to his back. Lieutenant Bradley watched him for a long time before he turned away, jogged out of his thoughts by the soft voice of Colonel Gibbon.

That one of your'n?

Yes, sir.

You tell him to go up there?

No, sir. I'd of gone m'self. I'm thinking maybe I should go anyway.

The hell you will. You better stay right here, son. We got a war to win come morning.

The Colonel shook his head and spat in the snow. He looked around at his troops in the gathering darkness. To a man they looked tired, shocked, desperate and getting on toward drunk. Huddled down in twos and threes against the cold, trying to get fires going, talking in low whispers. Some still calling out for help.

Gibbon reached for his flask.

We didn't lose much, really, Bradley said.

Yeah well, we sure did lose enough. Ever night out in this godforsaken weather's a strike agin us.

We'll have another shot at them tomorrow.

Yeah we will. The Colonel offered Bradley a drink. Did you git a look at that scene up on the hill?

Naw, but I got a good idea what it was.

Tell it, son.

We saw something similar when we passed back through Bighorn.

Did you now?

They set them up along there for us to find.

Set them up?

The Sioux set up crosses like that, with skulls dug up from the dead . . .

Dressed in Seventh Cavalry colors. Kinda makes you sick at heart, don't it?

I believe that's the idea, sir.

Guess so, whadya'all do?

Well sir, we shot em down.

You did?

Each and every one of them.

Good for you.

We didn't think on it or even talk about it much. It sure made us feel a lot better.

I spect it did at that. Was it Crazy Horse?

That was the Crow's idea, sir.

All right then, I'll see you later. We're going up there again at dawn. You go and find your other men.

Thank you, sir.

Bradley found Gentle and Comes Up Red by a fire. They were tending to a man with a broken leg.

Wassup, Cap'n? Gentle said.

Bradley nodded hello.

We got us a horse we done gutted, cooking on the fire. Join us for dinner, Cap'n.

Just like old times, hunh Gentle. Y'all all right?

A lot better than some of these other boys, Gentle grunted as he pulled on the man's leg. The fallen soldier let out a howl. Me and the Indian already set three broken legs. Those Sioux sure know how to mess with a man.

Crazy Horse, strong spirit, the Indian spoke up half Crow, half English. Who kills becomes Chief.

It's easier to understand ya when ya speak American, Gentle said, and poked at the fire, turned over the seared, smoking piece of flesh. Where's the German man anyways?

Bradley threw his head up toward the hill. The smell of the horse cooking made his bile rise, he was having a hard time getting words out of his mouth.

C'mon.

H-h-he went up after that man got shot up there.

You sent him?

H-hell no. He just said he was going. I couldn't order him not to.

You could a thought pretty hard about it.

I did.

You want to go after him, don't you?

Don't y'all?

Just waiting for orders, Cap'n.

It took near to an hour for all of them to make it up the slope. They had tied their horses in camp and went on foot. Each of them slipped and fell a couple of times. By the time they made it they were all of them soaking wet. They found Huebner underneath the crossed sticks. They were still smoking and charred black. Huebner had wrapped up the wounded man Ames in the blue coat left by the Indians. In one hand the dying man held the skull that'd been atop the cross.

This man's going to die, Huebner said quietly to the others.

Have you been able to do anything for him?

Keep him warm some, talked to him.

Where's he shot?

Just about everwhere.

Damn and he's still . . .

It's all right.

The soldier Ames let out a raspy whisper. His voice sounded like dying wind.

Ahh've made ma peace.

You were the only one to make it up here, Ames. You've done a brave thing.

I done and got m'self killed is what I done.

No, no I talked to Colonel Gibbon. He praised you highly, Ames, Bradley lied.

It's nice of you to say so, Cap'n. I preciayter y'all coming up here to see me off.

Y'all just rest now.

I guess I'll be seeing you fellers by and by.

You just rest, soldier.

Anyway, it helps to have y'all here.

They all stood up and looked around.

You seen any Indians up here, German man?

Naw, I believe they're camped there beyond the trees.

Hey, where's the Crow?

Did he come up here with y'all?

Sure he did.

Damn, he must have slipped off to have him a look'see.

Y'all don't wait much for orders anymore, do ya?

Ahh, Cap'n.

Well, let's have us a look around then. Huebner, why don't you stay here with Ames.

All right, sir.

They found the Crow Indian sitting under a cottonwood tree. He had a knife wound in his thigh bleeding pretty well. When he saw the soldiers, the Crow held up a string of four scalps. Blood dripped from them onto the snow. Bradley could hear it.

Damn, looks like old Crow man's been busy.

Comes Up Red smiled back at them, but Gentle and Bradley could see that the movement had caused him pain. That's when they saw the hole in the Indian's chest.

Where else they git you there, Crow man?

The Indian pulled back his coat to reveal a gaping wound just below his chest. It sucked and bubbled blood in and out as he breathed.

They stuffed the wound with leaves, mud and ice. Gentle cut the lining from his coat and they were able to wrap the Crow Indian's chest. Gentle helped him to his feet, but the Crow refused to be supported and walked on his own. He fell down a few times but then hissed at them when they went to help.

When they reached Huebner, Ames was dead. They fashioned a litter for the dead man out of branches and rope and took turns dragging him down the slippery draw. Comes Up Red fell often and by the time they got him back down he'd lost a lot of blood.

They made it back down to the camp a few hours before dawn. Lieutenant Bradley made a report to Colonel Gibbon. Huebner and Gentle, both exhausted from the events of the day, slept fitfully, Gentle with his finger in the trigger-ring of his trapdoor Springfield. The Crow Indian Comes Up Red did not sleep at all. His leg stiffened and his chest hurt every time he moved.

The other soldiers had spent the evening hours after the skirmish on the hill drinking and through the night they passed out in clumps around sloppy fires. Most did not even set up camp, but instead slept where they fell. And in the morning when they awoke they refreshed their thirsts with wake-me-ups they'd left in their bottles. They nibbled hardtack and chewed on scraps left from the horses.

In all, over eight hundred soldiers charged up the icy hill near Box Elder Creek. Beyond the crest of the hill lay the plateau about fifty yards square where the blue coat and skull had been set on the cross. They scaled the hill in waves. The officers drew lots and a West Pointer, Lieutenant Fox, led the first charge. He was shot in the groin in the first chaotic moments of the rush up the hill. He spent the next hour in screaming agony as his men struggled up the hill, many falling under heavy gunfire. The soldiers could not defend themselves. It was all they could do to keep a good hold, and not fall flat on their faces.

The Colonel's strategy was to keep sending men up the hill until eventually enough made it to the top to overwhelm the Indian forces. Of the first regiment less than half of the men made it to the plateau where the Indians waited for them and hand to hand combat ensued. The Sioux massed their forces at the crest. Women and children stayed back in the camp beyond the trees to the rear of the plateau. Once Fox's regiment had made a third of the way up the hill, Gibbon gave the order for the next group to follow. A pair of Hotchkiss guns were set up at the bottom to shell the Indian line.

The regiments that followed stepped over fallen comrades offering quick words of encouragement to the dying and prayers to the dead. Around eleven in the morning Gibbon sent a detachment of soldiers to clear the hill.

Comes Up Red was gone after the other three scouts came back from predawn reconnaissance. The Crow Indian left an indentation in the packed snow, colored pink with blood from where he'd spent the night. They looked but could not find him.

Maybe he went off somewheres to die, Gentle said.

Don't say that, Bradley answered.

What if it's the truth, Cap'n?

I've had about enough of that as I can stand, Huebner spoke up.

Huebner and Gentle had spent the morning in a support line, firing cover from the base of the hill. Bradley stayed at the Colonel's side and by his order sent each succeeding line into battle. It was hard for him to speak sometimes, and often he just waved his arm. The nervous soldiers got the message.

Bradley's shaking had begun as the casualties mounted on the hill. A charge from one of the regular's rifles knocked out the hearing in his left ear. At noon Gibbon called, Clear, for the officers to mount the hill. Bradley scaled the slope carefully with Gibbon but broke into a run maybe twenty feet from the top.

Where's he going?

He must see something.

If he ain't careful that'll be the last thing he does see.

Gentle gave a whoop and tried to follow Bradley, but he slipped, fell down, and lost sight of him, cursing his luck. They called for him, but the Lieutenant paid no mind.

When he reached the crest, he ran headlong into a skirmish. He'd been scared to almost paralysis and when he ran he had to: he was scared. A Sioux charged toward him war club raised. His eyes caught on a streak of red paint striped around the brave's chest. He aimed for it and pulled the trigger of his rifle. The bullet hit the man in the stomach. The brave gasped and bowed but did not stop.

Bradley met him halfway. He would remember the sounds for the rest of his life, the grunt of impact, his boots crunching the snow, his bayonet hitting rib, at once into the Sioux chest up to the hilt. The thrust brought them face to face. He could smell his dying gasp. Pine somehow, cut with gunpowder, mucus and blood. As Bradley fell, the blade became lodged in the brave's ribcage. Bradley almost lost grip of his rifle. He crouched with the fall then stepped on the Sioux's shoulder. The blade made a sucking sound as he pulled it out. Something made him turn in time to see a second Sioux with a rifle leveled at him waiting for him to rise enough to target. He ducked again quickly and the brave's shot grazed his right shoulder. The feeling there was wet and warm. Before he had time to think, he aimed his own rifle and shot the brave in the face. The bullet entered the brave's right eye and the charge exploded his face into a mess of bone and cartilage. Bradley saw his black checker-painted face the moment the bullet struck, and the amazing shower of blood that speckled the snow-covered branches of the pine the brave had jumped out from seconds before he died. Bradley reloaded, and took aim at another Sioux scampering out of the bushes and felled him.

All around the Sioux were now in full retreat. The battle at the plateau ended with the Indians fleeing a now overwhelming rush of soldiers clearing the crest with little or no resistance. Bradley spotted Huebner and Gentle running with a group of soldiers into the growth of trees toward the Indian encampment, and for a few long moments he just stood there watching. He brought his gun down from the shooting position: he wasn't shaking anymore at all.

The sun had never come out that day and the sky was gray through the morning into the afternoon. A constant cold wind blew, rustled and bent the tops of the trees.

Lieutenant James H. Bradley stood watching the few leaves left trembling. Other soldiers passed by him after clearing the hill, but none stopped to join him. He walked by each of the Indians he had killed. The first one was still breathing. He thought of Gentle, his admonition to prayer,

Father in heaven, he whispered under his breath,

Thine hands have made me . . .

Yet thou dost destroy me . . .

Job's words were just what came to him as he cocked his pistol and stopped the Sioux with a bullet to the head.

Thou hast made me as the clay;

Wilt thou bring me into dust again?

Before the prayer was done, he shot twice more.

At some point he wiped the blood from his bayonet on his pants. He walked down a path of sloshy mud and snow through the wood, passing by bodies of soldier and Indian alike. He kneeled by one soldier, a man with a full beard, and looked in his eyes as the man's life left them. When he made it to the village, the Indians that could had fled.

A circle of soldiers played with two wounded, disarmed braves. They kicked them back and forth around the circle, swinging at them with the butts of their rifles and taunting them obscenely. One soldier pulled down his pants and pissed at them. One Indian begged for mercy; the other steadfastly refused to speak.

Another group had three squaws, a mother and what looked like two daughters. They took turns mounting them and beating them about the face. The entire village was sacked, food burned and all ammunition stores shot off in a series of great and colorful explosions. The soldiers brought out their liquor and had their way.

Did you git their scalps, Cap'n? Gentle asked him.

No, Corporal, I did not.

Why not?

Well, they were already dead. I don't know. I didn't think of it.

The soldiers celebrated the victory in the abandoned Indian village through the night. Eventually though they ran out of liquor. They became cold and tired. They passed out drunk and woke up frightened in the dark cold. Some time in the early evening word spread that the Sioux wanted to talk. They might be willing to surrender to an Indian Agency.

They got no food, no bullets, said one soldier. It's the fucking dead of winter. What else they gone to do?

What about Crazy Horse? another asked. Has anyone seen him?

Bradley had found Comes Up Red in the woods after the skirmish on the plateau. Somehow in the last hours before dawn the Indian had dragged his wounded body up the hill. Bradley found him under a cover of leaves, his skin blued from the cold, struggling to keep warm. He got him up, and got him to a fire in the camp. Now as the word spread about the meeting with the Sioux, the Crow Indian insisted he had to be there.

Sure you can go, Bradley told him.

They took up the Indian on their shoulders and brought him over to where Gibbon and the rest of the command had set up their camp. The Crow could not speak above a raspy whisper. He kept waving his arms, making a circle and pointing at the moon. Every movement caused him great pain.

What is that crazy Indian man trying to tell us? Gentle said, still a little drunk.

He says the enemy must all come in at once. Before the next sunset, Huebner said. The other Crows from Gibbon's troop stood around solemnly.

He says we have to talk with the Chiefs.

My men are going to be starving out here by tomorrow, starving and cold, Gibbon said. I got half a mind jes to leave em all out here. Bradley, what do you think?

We can't just leave them out here. Take the men back. We can meet the Indians.

You and who else's army?

Everyone laughed.

Huebner and Gentle looked at their Lieutenant.

I guess it's happening again, fellas, Bradley said and swallowed. Someone handed him a canteen.

Hit's been a long day, Lieutenant, Gibbon spoke up. One way or t'other, we're leaving back for the fort come 'morrow. They can come with us, or we'll leave em out here to die.

The Crow Indians spent the night tending to and praying over their brother Comes Up Red.

When the army met the Sioux, it was on the wide open plateau. Foot deep snow and wet boots. Ten Indian braves came forward, with Crazy Horse in the lead. Most of the white men had never seen the great Chief before. He was painted completely red, braving the cold with a white bone shield draped over his shoulders and a loin-cloth. The others could be clearly seen behind them, massed in the trees. The woods hummed with a noise that caused the air to tremble. It was an awesome sight. They sounded off in this fashion for a full five minutes before the Chief raised his hand for a sudden silence.

That was when the Crow Indians opened fire.

Lieutenant Bradley ran out into the field first. Gentle and the other scouts followed quickly, shouting after him to stop. The Sioux emptied from the field once the shooting started; the trees, moments ago teeming with the presence of the Indians, were now quiet, as the Sioux left their wounded on the snow and disappeared into the deep woods. Bradley saw the blood before he saw the Sioux squaw. The red glowing through a line of sagebrush. As he neared at full sprint, he saw her black hair. He knelt by her side. Bradley grabbed up some snow and packed it into the gaping hole in her neck. Her eyes were wide open, rolled back in her head and then held steady. The blood gurgled in her throat, her whole body jerked then he heard a slight whistling sound, a catch.

She could breathe now. She closed her eyes and took a few, deep, grateful breaths.

When Bradley looked up, he saw the Crows then Gentle and Huebner. He saw one of the Crows kneel over a dazed and wounded Sioux. The Crow's knife flashed in the odd sunlight and he took the kneeling man's scalp. The Sioux's eyes bulged until they seemed ready to come out of his head. He raised his hands toward the bloody mess of his head then pitched forward, writhing in the snow, blood all over his hands. He wasn't dead. Another Crow ran toward Bradley and the fallen squaw. Huebner had knelt down beside the other two fallen Sioux warriors close to Bradley.

Gentle grunted, raised his rifle and shot it, hitting one of the Crows in the knee. The man crumpled in pain. The rest hesitated and Gentle waved his gun at them.

G'wan, he said. Party's over.

After a few minutes they backed off, cursing, blood running from their mouths.

Of the twelve Sioux warriors that fell in the Crow ambush, the scouts Gentle, Bradley and Huebner were able to save five, four warriors and Bradley's squaw. A few of the soldiers galloped into the woods to give chase to the retreating Sioux, but they'd gotten away. After the tumult in the field, it took a couple hours to regain order among the troops. In the early aftermath Colonel Gibbon gave the order for troops to begin a return march immediately to Fort Keough.

The three scouts stayed with the wounded. Gibbon dismissed the Crow scouts on the spot and told them all to go home.

They rode off together in the afternoon as the sun started to set and turn the land dark. They rode down to the creek, the six of them, watered their horses and headed for their homeland.

Gibbon found Lieutenant Bradley after the line of troops had already started the march back toward the fort.

Bradley, you're alive.

Colonel, I request permission to take these Sioux back to the Fort for proper medical attention.

Damnit, James, you took a helluva chance.

No one ordered those Crows to open fire.

No one ordered you to run out into the field like some goddamn Mary of Mercy either. You could have gotten yourself and your men killed. Hell you shoulda.

These Indians were surrendering.

Well shit, James, you can do what you want to. I've got to lead these troops back in.

The army left them behind. By the time they had made litters and hitched them to their horses, dusk had fallen. Colonel Gibbon had relented and dispatched a couple of troopers to help them. They were five, with one Indian apiece trailing behind in the snow. The soldiers walked the horses down the steep bank then went down to the water to wash in the icy waters of Box Elder Creek.

Are you sure we're doing the right thing here, Cap'n? What if those Indians came back looking for these uns?

What if they did?

I think we might be a little outnumbered, sir.

Private Gentle, I want to thank you for following me out there.

Cap'n, I b'lieve I'd follow you anywheres, you know that.

We've been through it, haven't we?

I just wish you wouldn't try so hard to git us all shot up like that. I kind of liked them old Crows.

So did I.

Cap'n, I'm a willing to keep on with this. But what are we going to do with them when we get them back to the fort?

There's a hospital there, ain't there?

If you say so.

The two troopers were also German like Huebner. One of them was sick and kept sneezing from a cold. The other was born in the old country, the same town as Huebner's parents in Germany. They talked about old days for a few minutes by the water. The cold came on them hard, and the wind so fierce all they could do was holler and stamp around.

Huebner built a fire. He found some boards from an abandoned wagon, used the buckboard as a shelter for the wind and then when it was going, threw everything on there. They were able to warm their hands and dry their socks and boots. Bradley unhitched his litter from the horse and dragged the wounded Sioux woman to the fire. He pulled the scrap of cloth, but it was bloody and stuck to her face. He had to wet it with water from the creek and gently pull it away. There was a film over her eyes and they were shot through with blood. Her face was flushed and hot to the touch, but her hands were cold and clammy. She flinched at the touch of the water, but showed no other signs of life. Her eyes were open but unseeing. He had to pull the wraps from her hands and hold them up by the fire.

Huebner also brought his Indian up to the fire and directed the other Germans to do the same.

Gus, I want to thank you for backing me up out there.

Ahh Hell, you're the Cap'n.

You know what I'm talking about. I wasn't acting as the Captain.

I'm with you, sir. I believe the army's done left us out here to die.

Bradley didn't answer. He spat into the fire.

You think we should ride out or try to make camp here?

I think we better keep going, Cap'n, Huebner said.

He brought up the two Germans to meet Bradley. One was named Karl Heinz and the other Hans. They both smelled like they'd been drinking all day, that and beans and bacon. Lieutenant Bradley could smell it on their breaths and coming up from their clothes. As if they had each emptied a bottle over themselves to keep away the cold. They were both wrapped up from head to toe. Hoarfrost stiffened the cloths on their faces and hung from their brows. All Bradley could see was their eyes.

Where's Gentle? Have you seen him?

I'm right here, Cap'n.

Maybe you'd like to mount up so we can get out of here.

Waiting on you, Cap'n.

They rode, following the creek on through the night, and when they stopped in the morning by a bend, Gentle's Indian was dead.

Looky here this un's frozen as a board.

You just let him die, Huebner said.

I'll be damned if I did. What you say, German man? Which side are you on?

Ain't no time to be talking like that, Huebner said. He looked at Gentle and turned to walk back to his horse.

I ain't killed nobody, Cap'n. Ahh hell, he muttered to himself. He unhitched the litter and dragged the dead Indian behind a bush. He left him there.

They washed up in the creek and Huebner built another fire. Bradley pulled the squaw next to the fire. He ran his hands down her legs to check for any broken bones. They were swollen and cold. She breathed heavily now and her eyes were closed. When he touched the dressing on her neck, she moaned and her eyes opened. He thought she looked at him. He wondered what she must have seen. He'd been in the field now for over a year. He couldn't even imagine what he himself looked like anymore.

There wasn't anything to kill and they had very little food between them. They made a breakfast of some cornmeal the Germans had in their packs. They mixed in water and salted ham then heated it up in their mess-kits over the fire. Bradley took his gloves off and held the hot tin pan in his hands until he felt them burning.

How are y'all Indians doing? Bradley asked.

Well, the couple that's shot in the legs I giss are going to be all right, far as I can tell, Huebner said.

They done got the bullets out in the field?

Yep.

And the other?

We got one gutshot and near dead, Huebner said.

You think he's going to make it?

I think we should just shoot him right now and put him out of his misery, Gentle said.

All right, Corporal Gentle. Thanky.

Don't push me, Cap'n, goddamnit. Maybe we should shoot him and throw him up on the fire for food.

Huebner went over and stood in front of Gentle.

What the hell you want, German man? I'm a standing right here.

Gentle threw his gun down in the snow. Huebner took his arm, but Gentle just turned and walked away.

When Bradley walked up to Huebner, the German was still breathing heavily. C'mon Gus, he said.

Gentle, Bradley called out. We ain't going to leave ya out here. We ain't going to stay either. You best c'mon now.

They hitched the litters back to their horses and when they rode on again, Gentle followed. He didn't want to be left alone. They walked the horses along the icy burbling creek, one man ahead of the other. On one side a pine-covered butte rose into the sky, on the other there was a field, with just a few brown burrs of sagebrush poking out through the snow. The sun never came out that day, or the next. They rode through the night and when they stopped it was to warm themselves by a fire. Huebner went to check on the gutshot Indian and when he came back he had blood all over his shirt, soaking his mittens red.

Cap'n, we got a problem here. This here Indian's running blood out of all sides.

Huebner, you all right?

It's just a flowing out here.

It's called a hemorrhage, Gentle spoke up. The man is dying.

Billy Gentle you come give us a hand or you shut up.

Together the three of them rolled the Indian into the shallow water of the creek. A high keening death song escaped from his lips. Fear opened his eyes wide. He flinched all over at the feel of the cold. The water turned pink with the man's blood. The two Germans stayed back by the fire with the others. Bradley shook his head and went to check on everything else. They could do nothing for the Indian, but still he did not die.

The bleeding stopped, Cap'n.

Is he breathing?

I believe he is, Gentle said.

Gentle wrapped up the wound. He cupped some water in his hands and splashed it over the Indian's face. Then he filled his cupped hands again and put them to the man's lips.

He coughed and then very weakly drank.

Gus, Gentle called out. C'mere and take a look at this. He ain't dead.

Huebner kneeled down and put his ear to the Indian's mouth.

He ain't dead, Gentle said again.

He didn't raise his voice or smile, nothing. He couldn't believe it.

Well he's a breathing anyhows, Huebner said, and shook his head.

You think he's just gonna go and die agin or what, Gus? Gentle asked. After all we gone and done.

How the hell am I supposed to know. I already thought he was dead.

Mebbe we should go head and kill him now.

I'm going to pretend you didn't say that.

What? It's cold out here. They're just a bunch of Sioux.

Y'know, Gentle, sometimes you jes beat all. You saved the man's life.

All right, fellas, we got to keep going so we all don't die out here, Bradley said. Hitch em to the horses, and let's ride.

You think we can make it back to the fort by morning, Cap'n?

Not if we stay here and talk all day we won't.

When they rode on something in Bradley's manner reminded Gentle of their first days out, right after the Custer massacre. We got our Cap'n back, he said to Huebner.

Sure as hell sounds like it anyway, don't it.

They made it into the camp before the next morning broke, five cold and hungry men, dragging the wounded Indians behind them on the litters. They rode straight through the gate to the hospital, and spent the night there, all of them, without even bothering to fall out or report to duty.

The next morning Bradley went to see Colonel Gibbon. When he walked through the door the Colonel jumped up and wrapped the Lieutenant in a bear hug.

You made it, he said.

You just left us out there.

Hell what was I supposed to do? I could of lost the whole damn army.

I know it, Bradley said, and nodded his head.

For a few dying Indians. Did ya bring them in?

Yes we did, sir. We got three Sioux warriors and a squaw.

What kind of shape they in?

Well they ain't dead. We lost another on the way over.

Gibbon shook his head and spat brown tobacco into the snow.

Just froze to death is all I guess, probably woulda happened anyway.

Anyway?

Nothing, sir. There wern't nothing that could be done.

I guess you b'lieve you had it tough out there.

I don't hold nothing against you, Colonel. I knowed you did what you had to.

Gibbon turned sideways, scuffing his boot on a rock.

To hell with you, Lieutenant, he said over his shoulder. Damnfire, next time you want to run out into a field after a bunch of fallen Sioux . . . well shit, Bradley. There wasn't nothing I could do. What you going to do now?

That's what I came here to ask you.

We ain't going anywhere for a while. Hell, you scouts are on your own, if you want to get out and look around, but this man's army is staying put until spring.

What about Crazy Horse and the Sioux?

Shit, they ain't got no food. They ain't got no bullets.

They'll be lucky to last the winter, sir.

Goddamnit, Bradley, you can't save the whole damn Indian race. That ain't what we come for anyways.

I guess so, sir.

The thing is, son, we're still catching hell from command back east. It was Crazy Horse, Sitting Bull and the Dull Knife Cheyenne what got Custer. We ain't got none of them

Sir, Crazy Horse and Dull Knife are starving in the cold. You just said that. Sitting Bull ran off to Canada . . .

Are they alive?

Yes, sir.

I don't think I have to tell you where we are and what we're out here for. After all you've seen.

Yes, sir.

Why don't you find your quarters, James. We can talk again, figure things out a little.

All right, Colonel Gibbon.

Shit, James, it's good to see you. Don't make it so hard.

I've always appreciated what you've done for me, sir. In all due respect I don't see how it could be any worse.

Bradley went back to the hospital before he found his quarters. He built a blazing fire in the place there and checked on all the Sioux. When he kneeled beside the squaw's bed, she opened her eyes and looked right into his. The film over them was gone. He

didn't know what to say. He patted her hand and when she didn't
withdraw, he took it in his and held her hand there for a moment.
She sighed then closed her eyes. When he let go of her hand, he fixed
the blanket. She turned over and went back to sleep.

Bradley ate a plate of stew he'd picked up at mess and then fell
asleep in the chair beside her bed. The doctor was a man named
Lonnie Johnson. He was older and always had a flask with him.
Bradley had awakened, and he watched the doctor walking quietly
from bed to bed. The floor of the hospital was dirt, and the doctor
held a candle in his hand as he walked. When he was done, he pulled
a chair next to Bradley's to join him in rest.

How they doing? Bradley spoke up.

Oh, you surprised me, sir.

Bradley stretched out and yawned.

How long have I been out?

Well it's the same day if that's what y'mean.

Shit, it's dark out.

It's past midnight. Lieutenant, maybe you should go on to your
barracks.

Hell, Doc, I ain't even found out where it is, yet. He looked over
to the bed. He didn't want to go anywhere. He felt better here. He
didn't want to be alone in his room.

She's doing real well, the doctor said, following Bradley's eyes.
That's a strong woman, there.

How old ya think she is?

Maybe twenty, maybe twenty-five. Probably about the same as
yourself.

What about the gutshot one?

He's messed up pretty good.

Where's he at? He ain't died has he?

No, sir, he ain't going to either if I have my way.

He nearly died when we had them out there. We just put him in the water. Hell I thought he was dead. I just walked away. It was all I could do at that moment. I didn't want to watch someone else die.

I know how you felt.

Next thing I knew he was all right. I guess the cold water helped.

Could a been. I'm as much a preacher as I am a doctor in a place like this. Well if you're going to be here, I think I might turn in m'self. There's coffee if you want some, Lieutenant.

Real coffee?

Yes, son, there's some already in the pot. You can just heat it on up.

Bradley sat up until dawn. Some time before, the Indian squaw started to call out in her sleep. She was dreaming. Bradley walked over and held her hand in his. When she quieted down, he sat down on the cot beside her until she rested again.

9

They spent the rest of the winter at Fort Keogh. When the great thaw started and shiny clear water ran down the colored walls of the canyons they were still there.

They drilled new recruits; they played ball in the snow, they drank, smoked, chewed tobacco and spit a lot. The men got a weekend of liberty at the Johnny Bowman ranch. They got drunk, gambled all night then spent the rest of their pay on house girls. Only Huebner had much experience with this. They found Gentle the next day in a puddle, clutching a pair of bloomers to his chest.

Gentle changed. Just like that, he was gone from all of them. He walked the grounds, sometimes Bradley would see him passing by the open door of the hospital, but Gentle never set foot inside, not once since they'd been back. Gentle took watch, sitting up in the crow's nest by the southern wall of the fort. Huebner would look for him up there in the dark; he couldn't see him though, sometimes just the fire-red lit end of his pipe like a tiny flare up against the dark.

It was when the melting started, finally, when they'd been back most of a month that Gentle started going for his rides. He disappeared for days at a time. Colonel Gibbon could have called him to account for it, but Lieutenant Bradley saw that he didn't. Sometimes Gentle would come back with game that he'd killed and give it to the cook at mess hall for dinner.

Who knows what he saw? The snows ran down the mountains in streams down the draws of the coulees, glistening in the sun that filled the valley with its yellow light, the water murmuring over the dirt and grass just at the level of hearing. He scrounged up a Bible from someone, from somewhere. The pages all cracked and falling out, sometimes flying off in the wind. When he was in the fort he sat for hours in a wooden chair in the corner underneath the guard-post, turning the pages, whispering. Other times he read aloud. His voice had deepened, his eyes set dark in the hollows above his cheeks. Sometimes men gathered in God's name to listen to Gentle read. He didn't preach or stray at all from the written word. When he was done, someone would usually pull out a mouth harp, a feller had a guitar. The songs would start but by then Gentle himself would be gone.

He would lead the target practice drills and this, if nothing else, kept him under orders and satisfied the command. He led the drills with his hard glare, his reputation and by the way he shot. He never missed, whether tin can, whittle stick, whether stationary or tossed in the air. He hardly spoke that anyone heard. He ate by himself in the mess at a chair pulled out from the line, away from the long wooden tables to the window. No one else sat like that, but no one said anything to Gentle either. Other than the Bible readings.

Huebner gave him a wide berth. They'd cross paths, at mess or in the yard. Huebner said howdy like always. Gentle might nod or might not. The German never held it against him. Once he was standing against the front gate-post, looking out through the open passage at the view over the long draw, past the long line of bristly scrub pines all the way down to the long blue river.

Gentle just walked right up to him, like the last he talked to him was yesterday.

What's up, German man?

Just watching the birds.

Oh yeah, what you seen?

Couple hawks, an eagle . . .

They're all out here, ain't they.

That they are.

You been talking to the Cap'n?

Sure, why not?

He never does step out of that hospital does he.

Course he does, Billy.

Not that I ain't seen. Gentle spat and rubbed it with his shoe. Maybe's he sweet on her, he said.

Mebbe.

C'mon, German man, she's an Indian. Hell, she's a Sioux. Things ain't like they was.

No, I guess not.

We done rode with him halfway across up and down this country-side and now he don't know us.

The Cap'n is right here. I talk to him near everday. He ain't going nowheres.

Naw, I guess not. It's just that . . .

Huebner looked at Gentle and waited.

I seen a man hung one time. I ever tell you that?

I don't b'lieve.

It were right afore church one day. The preacher and the hangman were one same feller. Long black coat man with a hat alike.

This was in down south?

That's right, German man. The Yadkin River. We all follered him down there. He walked right out into the water. Called out the folks to join him. Had the whole town out in that muddy river in their Sundee clothes.

Your folks too?

I was about fourteen. I had different places I could go, folks' barns and porches. No one had the heart to chase me away.

What happened to your'n, Billy Gentle?

Sometimes I think I don't remember . . .

Do you?

They hung that man then went to the river. Some say it was my daddy. I never knowed.

All right.

Gentle had his Colt out. He sighted a hawk with his arm straight out from his eye on the barrel, but he didn't shoot.

Gus, you got any idea when we might be going out agin?

Soon enough.

You ready?

Sometimes I think it'd be all right with me if I never shot another gun in my life.

You don't mean that. What else would you do?

Hell anything.

I don't know, sometimes I think my life was waiting to git started until I got out here. It's just like the man in the black coat said, in the Revelations part. There ain't nothing else after this.

Don't you ever wish you could go back home?

I would sleep in the church sometimes, in the pews. Ain't no one could chase me away there.

The first thing Bradley touched was her scar. She'd taken his hand and put it there, where the bullet had gone through her neck. Just lightly, her fingers passed his over the mark, sunken and soft. Bradley closed his eyes, his stomach all flutter and ice. He moved his lips to her and warmed them against her bare shoulder. From that moment on, her lips were open to his. She never left his mind again. He took her for walks when she was able. He brought her food in the hospital. Sometimes the cook would look at him, but no one said anything to his face. He waited for them to, but not one of them ever did. He slept in the hospital most nights, in the chair or in the extra cot open now since Jensen, one of the boys from the Box Elder Creek battle, died. He taught her English. Whenever she spoke her own language, he wanted to kiss her. Maybe it was the sound of the words, or that they came from her lips. Maybe it was the whole damn war. He didn't think it mattered. Except when she pulled away and got a far-gone look in her black eyes. They hardly knew what to do the first time. It was over before they knew it. A sweat had broken out on his forehead. She wiped it off with her fingers to her mouth. When she cried he wished he could. Nothing came, so he held her. He was not the kind of man who cried. His father had told him a long time ago that's what he would become. Now it's what he was. When they heard Doctor Johnson snoring at the end of the dark hospital barracks, they giggled together. The second time they took it easy and when dawn broke with the birds twittering outside they were still together.

James?

Yes, sir.

Gibbon had called Bradley in out of the rain, to stand on his porch under the dripping eaves.

Y'know we can't keep them Sioux here indefinite.

Sir?

We could move them to the guardhouse for a while, but sooner or later something's going to have to happen.

We could let them go.

James, they are prisoners of war. I ain't said nothing up to this point.

What do you have to say, Colonel?

Hell, son, I know it's lonely out here. Go 'head and keep the squaw for a while, what the hell. Can't say it ain't happened before.

It ain't like that, Colonel. I could marry her, what about that?

You can do whatever you want.

The Colonel took a drink.

Hell, James, he said, calm down here. I got word today that Crazy Horse has surrendered to Fort Robinson.

Naw.

Yes-sir-ree Bob. Him and his whole damn tribe. Starving, thin as sticks, with hardly even any ponies left. Red Cloud brought them in himself.

When did you hear this?

It just came over the wire. Thought you'd want to know. Maybe she wants to be with her people. Hell, I could send y'all over there. We're just sitting on our hands out here. You think about what you want to do.

Alright, Colonel, I will.

Huebner sat with his back up against the gate. He had taken off his boots to clean them. He was very superstitious about his boots. He'd gotten a pair of his own before joining up. Most of the troopers had the long black leather ones. They were good for wearing outside the trousers but the leather was thin, cheap and cracked easily. Huebner had gotten his specially made by a cobbler on

George Street, back home in New Brunswick. The sign said:
BOOTS MADE FOR SOLD-JERS.

He'd gone in and paid on trust for the six weeks from the time he
signed on to the time he left. His were lace-up with steel eyeholes
and rivets, and a tough base of rawhide saddle leather in the sole and
arch. They kept his feet warm and dry most of the time and though
he took some ribbing about regulations and the decidedly unflashy
appearance, he usually got the last laugh on the long hauls. When
others got frostbite, went begging or had to scrounge from the dead,
he just kept walking. He had a big foot, size thirteen, which was why
he thought to get them from the cobbler in the first place. That and
the sign.

August always liked signs. It was a sign that got him here in the
first place. All in all he figured it as one of the smartest things he'd
done in this man's army, bringing his own boots with him. They were
still in pretty good shape, scuffed up from all the riding and marching and dusty trails, with a deep cut across the top from one of his
spurs. Sometimes he found nails in the soles that he'd walked on, but
they never made it through the sole. Most of the nails he pulled out
were bent, the old cobbler's leather being tougher than the cheap
metal nails. He remembered the old man, an Italian named Ski-lino,
must have been eighty-five years old with a graying beard. He still
had all his hair and was very proud of it. Huebner never went into the
shop when the old gentleman wasn't pounding away with his hammer, nails into shoes, rivets out flat, or just a piece of leather. His skin
was like that.

He was hunched over for all the pounding but when someone
came into the shop, someone with business, he would haul himself
up ramrod straight and start talking, the old gentleman loved to talk.
He was one of those men who could not stop working. Once he told

Huebner the story of his family's passage to America. Huebner loved this part about his town, so many people from so many different places. No one had any problem telling him the tale of their journey. He had a way of listening and an honest, no account smile that could disarm anyone in seconds. If he didn't know the language, he would just smile with his teeth until the other had to join him.

The old Italian, Call me Joe, he said, kept a pencil drawing of his dear departed Louisa on his wall, and a pot of tomato gravy with sweet sausage and meatballs on a pot belly stove simmering at all hours. If you weren't hungry, when you came in, for a sandwich with fresh bread, he got this hurt look on his face. He was an easy touch for all the scruffy kids who ran the streets, and always welcomed them in for a meal. He'd told him to keep the shoes oiled down. That was the main thing. He'd gotten some animal fat from the cooks, and although it didn't always smell too good and would get the wild dogs to yapping at his feet sometimes, he always followed the old gentleman's directions.

So Huebner was sitting on his haunches, rubbing down his boots by the front gate that day when he saw the new troop filing in. They didn't look fresh, but they sure looked good, the Captain at the head of the line on a dappled gray and white quarterhorse looked positively elegant. Huebner sat and watched the whole troop pass through spit and polished, feeling a little sheepish, a poor cousin, with his tin of animal fat. Across the parade grounds he saw Gibbon, the one-armed General called Howard and a line of officers greeting the new troopers. He heard they came all the way from the Capitol in Washington, D.C. He saw Bradley step up and greet the Captain. They looked like old friends.

Bradley hadn't seen Perry since his days at West Point. Perry had been an upperclassman, one of the true shining lights of the officer school. Now he was General Howard's favorite son. He had started and captained the football team at the academy. He and Bradley sat down to drinks after a more formal dinner. Bradley received the Captain in his quarters, one of the adobe-walled cabins that had a woodstove, a couple chairs and a bed.

After the Sioux had served them their whiskeys she sat down in a chair next to Bradley. She'd been with him in his quarters since she'd left the hospital.

You must be doing pretty well, what with a servant and all.

She's not a servant, David.

She is an Indian?

She's a Sioux. Her name is Snow Melts.

Perry took a sip of his drink.

Well hell, James, she makes a good drink anyways.

When Perry smiled at Snow Melts, she looked back at him and her eyes softened. Bradley felt a wash of gratitude for his old friend.

So I hear you been getting around pretty good, James.

Yeah, you could say that.

You were at Little Bighorn. What was that like?

Wasn't pretty.

I saw your name in the papers all the way back east. You fellas were the talk of Washington. We wouldn't have gotten this far in the campaign without y'all.

You were in Washington?

Yes, as a special envoy to President Grant.

You met the Gen'l Grant?

Shit, James. Save that for somebody else.

So you were in on all the meetings, with the Chiefs?

They all came through. That's why we're out here now.

Yeah?

Seems like the Nez Perce are ready to say Uncle. General Howard's waiting for the word so we can go out and meet them to talk terms. Now that Crazy Horse is at Fort Robinson and Sitting Bull has run off to Canada they are pretty much the last ones. Things seem to be closing up pretty nicely.

Snow Melts shot him a glance; he saw Perry notice it too.

So Sitting Bull is in Canada? We heard that out here, but you never know.

That's the word we got. Run tail and hide.

Perry wasn't southern or country, he came from New York, but sometimes he liked to use the words and phrases anyway. He thought it made him sound more like a soldier. From what Bradley had heard his old friend was very popular with his men and never asked them to do anything he wouldn't do himself.

What are they going to do with all of them?

The Indians? Send em down to the Territory, what we don't kill. Perry looked at the squaw and took a drink. South of Kansas.

I guess they figure that'll solve it.

Won't it?

It ain't what they make it to be out east I know that.

It's been killing me sitting in Washington. I can't wait to get out there. What else you been doing? Did you run across Sitting Bull?

I guess Custer did. Maybe in Dakota Territory too. We sure fought off someone after that American Horse thing. We been keeping busy.

C'mon James . . .

Perry and Bradley talked until late in the night and shared a bottle of rye. After Snow Melts excused herself and went to bed, Bradley told his friend the story of their meeting.

You got some guts there, friend.

That or I've just gone crazy.

I'm glad you said it, James.

Perry wasn't smiling. I heard you had some bad times.

Shit, to hell with that. Less you been out there you don't know what it's like. We come out here thinking the Indians are all dogs . . .

Oh c'mon, James . . .

No you c'mon.

You're going to tell me you love an Indian, a goddamned Sioux no less. Hell, you should be shot.

Then shoot me. You don't know what it's like. Sometimes I just wish the whole damn country would go to hell. I came out here one way and I almost lost my damn mind out there in the snow.

James . . .

No, David, just let me talk. Maybe that's why I have her here. Maybe it's not fair to her. I'm sure you don't care. Everybody just calls her my little squaw whore. I just wish they'd all go to hell. And tomorrow when I'm sober if you act like you ever heard any of this, I'll shoot you.

Ahh hell, James . . .

Just try me. You want to know what it's like to be out here?

I got eyes.

It ain't something you see, Bradley said.

He wished that he had the right words to put it all down. Then maybe he could know it all himself. He wished he could describe for someone else the place he'd entered back there, the one that changed so many times in the past year. All he knew was that it was somewhere he could never turn back from.

Bradley caught himself and looked around.

Shit, Dave, I'm drunk. You caught me with my Sioux whore and got me drunk.

I'm a little loaded myself. Why don't we call it a night.

       She'd been running away since she'd been able to walk again. The first time she acted like she was sleepwalking. He had found her all the way down by the river. A trail worn down by the buffalo. He followed where long lashes of grass high as his shoulders had been matted down by her steps. She had kneeled down by a place where the river wound silver in the moonlight. The soldiers had built a wood footbridge nearby, cut from the thicket of cottonwoods. Bradley sat down there to wait for her. She knew he was there.

She came back each time, but she also left a piece of herself out there, beyond the walls of the fort. It wasn't something they could talk about.

This time after Perry left he found her waiting for him in the dark. He saw the glow of her calico dress, the one he'd gotten for her and she always wore, sitting up and waiting for him.

He told her what he knew about her people. Though he was drunk as sin when he'd lain down, the alcohol now just made it easier for him to face her and tell her everything. He felt better really, to have it all out. He had thought he loved her, but he didn't know how to say this. He tried to tell her some of the things he'd said to Perry. He didn't really understand a lot of it himself anyway. She was angry at first, as she slowly understood what had happened. He told her also about the details of the battle at Box Elder. How it had left her people. He also told her about the food and the bullets. The anger turned to tears and in the end, pride.

I can take you back, if you want to go, he said to her.

She just glared at him.

Want you, she said. What you want?

She got up, walked to him. She took his face in her hands and pulled him down with her into the coarse wool blankets on the bed. It was the only thing they decided.

We are not who we are, she said.

For a while no one knew that Gentle was gone. Huebner had gone out with him a couple times. They'd just ridden around through the great wide open land folding on to the distant mountains to the south. They pulled up in a dry water wash with cottonwoods hanging down to the sandy dirt, spent the night in the wild country out beyond the river. Pretty grasslands, hot, stark sandstone shelves, cut trails over the high plains; they had it all to themselves.

This is what it must have been like to be an Indian, Gentle said.

You think?

I don't know. I been trying to work some things out. I don't know shit anymore, Gus.

You'll be ready to ride when the time comes.

We'll see.

Huebner didn't suspect that one day Gentle would not come back.

You got your'n ready to ride? Gibbon asked Bradley out in the yard.

They been ready every time so far, sir. We been sitting on our hands for a while now.

Well, that's about to change. Gen'l Howard wants to mount an expedition.

Yes, sir.

We'll need you to ride out in the morning.

What's happened, Colonel?

We expected to get word of a surrender today.

From the Nez Perce? Perry told me about that.

Well, they changed their minds.

Sir?

We got word today they killed a bunch of townspeople down Clearwater way.

A raid?

I guess. Anyway, Howard wants to send his boy out first. Wants him to get his feet wet.

Think it'll be that easy, Colonel?

General Howard does. I ain't in charge of thinking anymore since he showed up.

I see what you mean.

The thing is, James, I want you and your boys to go with him.

We can do that.

Bradley found Huebner at the stables.

Seen Gentle?

Naw, not today I guess. Probably off somewheres mooning around.

Well, rouse him. We're going out in the morning with Perry's troop.

That's quick.

We got hostiles.

Huebner checked Gentle's bunk in the enlisted men's quarters and asked around, but he could not turn up their third.

What do ya think, Gus? Bradley asked when Huebner reported back to him.

His bunk's empty.

He didn't sleep there much anyway did he?

Naw.

When was the last time you were out with him?

Bout a week ago I guess.

Well shit. We'll go out either way, then.

Is this gonna be a problem, sir?

If he doesn't show up he's a deserter. You can get hung for that, Gus. Damn kid.

This ain't going to look good is it, sir?

Naw it ain't. Well, get your personals right to ride. We go at dawn.

Yes, sir.

Bradley went for a walk outside the fort before they left. The sky was blue with the coming dawn. He looked far over the rolling coulee and butte rises. The dew wet the wildflowers, and their sweet fragrant scents filled the air. He watched a flock of sparrows alight from a thicket of willows all at once as the first sun cut through the branches and lit up a cyclone of windblown dust.

10

There was no town. There was just a cottonwood tree where the townspeople had begun to gather. The lightning flashes of a far-off storm echoed silent vibrations over the hills. One of them held a green dress. He waved to the Captain in greeting as he rode up with Bradley and Huebner at the head of the long line of troopers. This man was named Grimes,

Artimus Grimes, he said.

He held up the dress to Captain Perry. He showed him the rip that went all the way down the front. He was shouting at Perry and the others long before they could make out what he was saying. When they were close enough to hear, the man, perhaps embarrassed now, stuffed the dress into his jacket.

We know right where they are, he said. When you go in there, you got to let us go with you.

He had a scraggly black beard and was dressed Sunday formal with a white collared shirt and black coat. When he addressed the soldiers he took off his hat.

A full regiment of over one hundred troopers had ridden through the night and into the beautiful green of southern Montana. They rode seventy miles in twenty-four hours, leaving at dawn and arriving as the new sun burned the blue mist off the dusty hills. When Perry got down from his horse the men of the town were upon him.

Now, now, he said. Calm down. I need someone I can talk to. I can't listen to all of you at once.

Captain Perry gave the order for the rest of the troopers to convene on the hillside. He left his Sergeant and Huebner in charge and went with Bradley to the tree. There was a bare spot at its base, where the roots came up out of the earth.

Why don't some of us just sit down right here, Bradley called out. I guess y'all know where the Indians are.

Grimes was still too angry to talk. His face was bright red, and Bradley couldn't help noticing the vein that stood out on his forehead. Bradley purposefully bent down and picked out a long strand of grass. He plucked it off to chew on. He tried to keep his hands from shaking. A couple times the man called Grimes pulled out the dress again. He held it out to the officers. But what could anyone say to that?

Another man spoke up. They came to my house after they left the Grimes Place.

What's your name, sir? Perry asked.

I'm Black, he said. There was a rain in the air. I smelled them coming in on the breeze. Like a bunch of wild damn dogs. There were a few odd sounds and then there they were. I didn't even have a chance to get my gun.

Perry started to ask a question, but Bradley reached out and touched his arm.

They let all my horses go. They killed one of the cows right there.

Slit its neck and left it there. I saw all this later. I live here on my own. I left my wife back in St. Lou-sis thank the Lord.

Did they, take anyone? Perry whispered the last word.

Naw they didn't hurt anyone, didn't hurt anyone a'tall.

They killed all the cattle though, and let all the horses to run wild, another man spoke up.

This one had a red beard and blue eyes.

My name is O'Donnell. We're out here all on our own.

Didn't hurt no one? Hell. This was Grimes finally finding his voice. They did this. He held up the dress, he couldn't find the words. They did this and they rode in a circle around my Dorothy. She hasn't stopped crying since. There wasn't a goddamn thing we could do about it.

Did you shoot at them? Bradley asked.

Damn right I did. But they were gone before I could get a good shot. They pulled the heads off of all ma chickens. They broke every single egg in there.

Your wife was unhurt?

Grimes just looked at him. He started to speak and then stuttered.

I wouldn't ast him that, Black said. Let's just leave that alone.

She's safe now though? Perry asked.

No one answered.

Bradley saw the other men gathered up on the hill. They all had their rifles with them. They were on foot. When they looked back at him, he turned away. It was something about their eyes. He couldn't hold what they had in them.

Do y'all know where they are?

The Jackson boys, Black gestured at two teenagers with big dirty hats. They follered em when they rode off. They say they're holed up in a camp near White Bird Creek.

How far is that?

At least a full day's ride I'd say, the one called O'Donnell said.

We've organized a militia, here, Grimes spoke up. When you go, Cap'n, you got to take us with you.

We can make y'all deputies right now, sir. We're going to need you to guide us over there anyway. How many of them were there?

It's hard to say. We think the camp might be bigger than what came out here. Maybe a hundred or so.

Hell, I think you boys must have them outnumbered at least three to one anyways.

Lieutenant Bradley took the Captain's arm. Perry, can I have a word with you?

Sure, James. 'Scuse us a moment, he said to the townsmen.

Captain Perry, you sure we need to take these men along?

What do you think?

They want blood's what I think. They ain't soldiers. That's a posse.

That ain't a bad thing. You want to tell them to stay here?

You are the commanding officer.

That's right. We'll let them lead us to them, then we'll see, James. Perry turned back to the townsmen. Have y'all had any trouble before? he asked.

Nothing like this. We've only all been out here for about a year or so. Black's been here the longest.

It's the Nez Perce all right, Black said. Chief Joseph is their leader. We always knew they were out there. But they never been a trouble-some breed.

Why now?

Black just looked Perry up and down.

Well shit, Cap'n, Black said. I guess them Indians know what y'all come out here fer. I wouldn't expect them to be that stupid.

We're out here to protect y'all citizens, Perry spoke up. We're out here to accept the unconditional surrender of their lands.

Black ignored him and spoke to Bradley.

I think it's the younger ones. I think this is their way of saying they're going to stand and fight.

You got any opinion about how we should handle this? Perry spoke up.

How we should handle what? Grimes sputtered. We need to ride over there and show them all whose land this is. I got a deed from the government. If y'all can't protect us, it's like the Captain here says, What the hell is that worth? I was in the States war, by God I'm a 'merican citizen out here.

Hell we were all in the war, O'Donnell spoke up.

All I'm saying is that fighting them Indians ain't the same. Black took a chaw from his pants and stuck it in his mouth.

What the hell are you saying?

They ain't going to be lined up in no formation I can tell you that.

What do you think, James? Perry asked.

We're going to have to wait and see how they're laid out.

They're up on a ridge, the boys said. Overlooking the White Bird Creek.

Do you know the way to get behind that ridge? Perry asked. That's the way we're going to have to go. Look, folks, we're going to ride out in an hour. Y'all git together what you can, he said to the three men from the town. Y'all can all ride out with us. He looked at Bradley, and motioned him to the side.

James, what do you think?

I think we can do better than to follow a couple of kids. Huebner and I could ride ahead and have a look.

I would rather you two stay with us, Perry said. He wiped his brow, and squinted into the sun.

Bradley said, You're the Captain.

Thank you, James.

Bradley patted his friend on the back and they walked toward their horses.

The field laid out long and wide. A warm breeze blew the tall grass over in waves like water. White aspen trees stood up tall on either side. In the distance the tall ridged butte. Bradley sent Huebner out with a couple others who came back with the word that the Indians were camped on top of it. On the other side and below lay the creek. They listened to the story of the two boys with hats too big for them and formed their plans by it.

They came in the back way. The trail they rode was hot and dusty. Bradley would remember how thirsty he was. He was reaching for his canteen when he saw the first puff of smoke. There was no report, it was lost in the sounds of the horses and the men. They were all mostly joking and talking after the long ride. No one thought anything would happen out here. No one had any idea that many of them had come to this place to die. All at once there were the puffs of smoke and the men started falling. The local men Black, O'Don-nell and Grimes were at the head of the troop with Captain Perry and his Lieutenants. Out of the ten or so at the head of the line, Bradley saw maybe seven of them go down right away.

The one called Artimus Grimes hollered, I'm shot.

There was a spot of blood on his dirty blue shirt. When he turned toward the place where his death came from he was hit again three or four times, in the cheek, both arms.

No one saw the Indians, just the puffs of smoke from their guns, from behind the aspen trees. The ones that could tried to get off a few shots, but there wasn't anything to aim at for the trees. Most of the men just broke and ran for their lives. When Bradley saw Huebner go down he felt his heart go with him.

He squeezed off a couple shots from his Springfield rifle, but it was more out of anger than any intent. Nothing could be done. Bullets whizzed past his ears like angry bees. All over sounded the cries of the hurt, the sudden dead. Huebner was too far away, there was no way Bradley could get to him.

Perry kept calling out to his men. He called out a name, a man would go down. His voice kept sounding higher and higher, all high and keening like something caught on a fence. You could hear he was scared. He sounded like a girl.

It's such a mess, he heard Perry calling to him. Every man for himself, the Captain said, as if there could be some order to all this chaos.

Bradley called out for Huebner, but he got no answer.

When Huebner's horse went down he kneeled down between its legs. He could see the shots coming from both sides. His leg hurt where he'd been shot and he kept cursing to himself

Goddamn,

    son of a bitch,

        every time he squeezed off a shot.

He saw one of the men from town, the one with the red beard, crawling toward him, then someone trampled right over him in the dust. Huebner tried to rise to reach him, to crawl if he had to, but he couldn't. His leg was numb.

Goddamn, he said to the man. Keep coming.

He was still alive. The man stood up right there, a bullet hit him right in the chest and he fell. Huebner heard his ribs crack from the impact. He dragged the dead man's body next to the horse and laid on his belly.

What good will I do anybody if I'm dead? he said to himself.

He didn't like that the man's eyes were open still, made his heart feel all cold and wrong, so he reached over with his fingers and shut them one at a time. Somewhere he could hear the Lieutenant, calling his name. He tried to answer. He didn't think anyone would hear him, but it did feel better to try. The dust from the trail choked his lungs. The air was filled with it, and the smell of the gunpowder and fear. The sweat that ran down his back felt cold. The man he hid behind had shit his pants when he died and he could smell it now. His horse was still alive. It whinnied high and loud and tried all at once to rise. Huebner yanked at the reins to pull it back down. He didn't want to be exposed to the gunfire from both sides. Maybe he should just let it go. If he died then maybe it would be all right to live.

But no one thinks of all that, he thought to himself. And he knew what it felt like to face death, to go crazy with fear and to do anything, anything at all to keep himself from dying. He cursed out loud to himself, and kept trying to aim at the places where he saw the little clouds of smoke.

It's bad enough to have to die out here, without having all those crazy thoughts running through his head.

The horse tried to rise again and this time he let it go. But it fell again then and it was dead.

The soldiers kept shooting after the Indians for maybe fifteen minutes, after they'd all gone. This was how Bradley saw it anyway.

There was so much confusion and awfulness, then all at once the Indians weren't there anymore.

For a second he wondered if they were really there at all. But it couldn't be the trees that had shot all the men. They couldn't have just all fell down and died. Perry said these things to him when he walked up, casual as a holiday, with a tremble in his voice that made him say each word twice, that made his legs all rubber when he walked. He tripped and fell right at Bradley's feet.

There wasn't nothing you could do, Dave. It ain't your fault, son.

Captain Perry looked all white. He nodded his head a couple times then he just fainted out cold in the grass. Bradley left him there and went to look around.

That's when he saw Huebner, just twenty yards away, standing in the middle of the trail with his leg bent in a funny way, like he was half-crippled. Bradley waved to him and called his name. It felt funny, everything had gone quiet. There was noise but it was like it was from another place. Everything was quiet. Up in the trees crows cawed. But their calls sounded all tinny. Bradley stuck his finger in his ear and it came down wet, like he'd been swimming, but instead of water there was blood. It didn't hurt though and he didn't bother to wrap it. It seemed like it took a long time to walk over to Huebner. He was so happy to see him alive.

Damn, son, I thought they got you, I really thought they did.

Corporal Huebner just looked at the Lieutenant, shouting. . . . Had he snapped again? he wondered. Why is he yelling? Then Huebner saw the blood in Bradley's ear. Huebner felt himself crying and all he could do was grab the Lieutenant up in his arms and give him a hug.

Goddamn, Cap'n, goddamn, he said. He started shaking in

Bradley's arms and he was heaving with tears. They stood there together, arm in arm among the dead and dying. They held as hard as
they could.

    They might as well have come out of the sky. Bradley was
petting a trembling horse and Huebner tending to one of the fallen
and wounded men when the Nez Perce came back down the dirt
face of the butte. It was all the three of them could do to run for their
lives. The sun had come down to the tops of the trees, bleeding red
through the leaves. It was still hot. When Bradley wiped his hands on
his pants they left a wet spot from the horse. He heard their calls, raw
and unearthly like a hundred birds descending from the sky. He saw
them first in the eyes of the man Huebner attended to. His eyes
widened and he pointed back toward the mountain. When Bradley
turned, he saw the cloud of dust, vibrating with the cries of the
braves moving down the mountain like a storm.

We have to make it to the river, Bradley said.

The German looked at all the other men, those that had already
broken off on their own dashes through the trees. He saw a man
crawling behind a tree. He saw him kneel down behind it and close
his eyes. Huebner saw his lips moving and guessed he must have
been praying.

Huebner!

Bradley grabbed his shoulder and yanked him toward the horse.

Let's go!

Bradley held out his hands clasped for Huebner to lean on.

Can ya boost that one on to the horse? Grab him and let's go.

What about the rest of them?

C'mon there ain't nothing we can do. Get on the horse.

Huebner grabbed up the man and threw him over the horse's

back. He stuck the boot of his live leg in Bradley's hands and hauled himself up. The other leg, numb-dead at his side, pulled along the flank and came to life with pain. He had to push it to the side with his hands before he could get astride the horse. Bradley gave the horse a smack and sent them off in the direction of the river. He ran to another horse standing, head down, over its dead rider, eyes rolling in fear, the hair on its back pricked. He grabbed the man's gun, jumped the horse and rode back to find Perry. He had his head in his hands. He didn't even raise it until Bradley kicked his hat off.

Wait, Perry said.

C'mon, man.

We got to make a stand.

No, we ain't.

Bradley jumped down and grabbed his friend by the shoulders. Perry crumpled like a sack of beans. His face looked ashen and drawn. When Bradley took him in his arms he got a whiff of urine that reminded him of a baby. It was a strange second that was past and gone into his memory. There wasn't any time.

They're gonna be on us.

What about my men? Perry said

What can, will, Bradley said.

He jumped on the horse and kicked with both boots. The horse jumped into a gallop; he had to grab on to the long hair of its neck and hold on. When they made it to the river the cold water revived Perry. He was able to hold on to the horse by himself. Bradley paddled on beside, jumping up when his boots lost touch with the muddy bottom of the river. He held the rifle over his head. Behind him he heard the pitiful cries of the men who weren't able to run.

Huebner waited when they reached the other side and yanked them out one at a time. The first few Indians had reached the river.

Huebner took potshots at the ones in the water and turned the river pink with their blood. The rest of them stopped short at the edge of the water and shot a few volleys toward the men scrambling for their lives on the other side. The men that could, shot back at them, from behind bushes and trees, from rocks and dales. Arrows flew over their heads or fell short and plunked in the water.

Are we alive?

The wounded man that Huebner had carried over spoke up from beside Bradley's leg.

We might as well be.

Did we make it?

Bradley aimed his shots over the heads of the retreating Indians.

Five or six of them had already fallen into the river rapids and had been moored in between the boulders. The rest were headed for the field of aspen trees. Only the tip of the red sun shone over the butte and the last of its light kissed onto the surface of the water and turned it the color of wine.

It's all right, Bradley said to the man beside him. We're safe over here.

How many of us are we?

About half I guess.

That ain't too good. That's pretty bad.

The sun's almost gone, Bradley said.

He took off his hat and ran his hand through his hair. He thought of Snow Melts. He wished the hand were hers. He wondered if she would still be there at the fort, if she were waiting for him to come back. A growth of red weeds stuck out of a sand marsh. The men took cover here between the river and a gradual grassy draw up the face of a coulee cut mountain rise. A gauze of clouds covered the moon's light and colored everything earthly the palest blue.

I'm all wet, the man said. I'm wet and I'm cold out here.

Bradley took off his coat and held it out to the man.

That's all right, Cap'n. You done enough for me today. A Baker ain't a man to forgit.

You'd of done the same, soldier. That your name?

Yes, sir. Andrew George Baker.

Where you from?

Pennsyl-tuckee, sir, right about where the one hits the other.

You hurt bad, Baker?

I believe I will live, sir.

He looked himself over in a way that made Bradley smile, despite everything. He couldn't help it. God, he needed a smile.

That's good, Baker, that's good. Here, why don't you sit tight. I better take a look around.

A few more men straggled over to their side as the dark came on.

They just let us go, one of them said.

He had a look on his face that kept away further questions.

They took some of our guns. Then they just let us go.

We had to hold each other up just to walk, his buddy said and shook his head.

By midnight the men had built a fire and Bradley counted fifty-seven survivors. All of the townspeople but the one named Black were left on the other side.

They're all dead, Black said. They just picked us all off. God it was awful.

Anyone who asked him he said the same thing. He had a flask of corn liquor and got good and drunk.

We can hold them off here, if they try to cross we'll pick em off like flies, a man named Salvatore said to Huebner.

Yeah, but if we move we're in trouble. We can only go up the rise. They could pick us off climbing up the hill.

I see what you mean.

They could run us down then. We ain't got enough horses. Wouldn't be pretty.

When Bradley asked for volunteers to ride and find Gibbon's army, Huebner raised his hand.

What about that leg, Gus?

It'll feel better when I'm a ridin.

Are you sure? I know you and trust you, but . . .

That's enough of that, Cap'n.

Lieutenant Bradley sent out Huebner with the one named Baker from Pennsly-tuckee. They were both hurt, but they could ride. If someone didn't come back with Gibbon quickly, there wouldn't be anything left for them to save. Huebner wanted to go and he was the only one Bradley knew enough to trust. The rest of the men foraged for food and did what they could for the wounded. They traded shots with the Nez Perce across the river.

Huebner and Baker stopped their horses at a place where the creek cut turned into a thin line through a high walled gorge. They followed alongside where it cut low through two gigantic mountainsides, then finally fed into a giant lake with fog garlands on the surface of the water that hid the fish they could hear jumping. Bright blue water, rainbow patterns off the water, sparkling sand and white dirt, stone of the rising gradated ridge that mirrored the colors of the sunset above their heads.

Place like this makes you feel small, Baker said. Makes a man think about God.

I guess he's been here, Huebner said.

It's all I was thinking about when we were out there.

The Indians pray too, y'ever heard that? Something about Baker brought out the devil in Huebner.

God is greater, Baker said, half to himself, half so Huebner would hear him.

You think they're praying to the devil?

I don't know. I know what my daddy would say.

Who's your daddy?

Sunday sermon preacher man, of the First Christian Church of Susquehanna County, Pennsyl-tuckee.

What do you mean Pennsyl-tuckee? Ain't it one or t'other?

That's what we call it. That's what it is. Do it have to be written down?

You think about this a lot?

I think about it all the time. My mama, my teachers they told me I should stop sometime.

Baker winked and let loose his goofy smile. But I can't help it, he said. It's just something I got to do.

They stopped now and again to let the horses drink from the creek. The trail was still treacherous for riding and it did them well to keep down the loneliness, so they kept up their talking as they rode.

All ma life I heard folks tell they stories, the day, the hour they let God, Jesus into their lives, Baker spoke up. I done tried and tried and I ain't seen him. I want to see him, I want to see his face.

Ain't that enough, to try?

No, it ain't. It ain't enough for me.

Mebbe, it's going to have to be.

Huebner kicked his horse. They came to a bend in the river and let the horses tread over a shallow place to the other side. They stopped in a field of wild daisies and watched as the horses brushed their noses through the petals.

Was yesterday your first?

Battle?

Yeah.

It was and I almosted died. Maybe God's trying to tell me something about ma faith.

You think he's going to protect you out here?

Might take me to a better place if I was'ter to die, I hope.

That's some hard thinking you been doing, Baker.

I know, he said. He smiled his boy's smile. It keeps me up sometimes.

I can see how it might.

They say y'all was the ones what found Custer dead.

We found whatever was there. We couldn't tell who was who.

Naw?

Naw.

You think they're going to be all right back there?

I don't think about things like that.

Shit, I wish I could be like that.

The men stranded at the river ate what was left in their packs. They shared whatever they had all around. By the second night it was gone. Hardtack, salty ham, hard beans and what else. They started looking at the horses. Perry seemed a lot better. He tried to apologize to Bradley but he just told him, That'll be enough of that.

Lieutenant Bradley met the Indian out in the water. Dusk neared, the crows cawed in the high leaves of the stand of aspens. Hundreds of flies buzzed in their faces and lighted onto the cattails. When they saw the Indian walk up across the river from them, it was a few minutes before any of them thought to raise a gun.

Don't get any crazy ideas, Bradley said. Let em come.

Hold your fire, men, Perry echoed. You're the one that knows the Indians, James.

Bradley wanted to punch him. He never thought Perry would be like this when the time came. But then you never knew. Maybe he'd do it later. Maybe it would help.

I think I'll do that, Bradley said.

He stepped into the cool river water. Neither wanting to defer nor offend the other, they walked to a shallow spot where the rapids ran white toward a bend. There was a run of rocks and the stepping across them was not too hard. The Indian wore skin pants and boots with a bright blue shell, and a dyed bone battle shield hung over his bare chest. He had a bow strapped across his back and a hacked off rifle in a holster next to his thigh. His eyes were green, cut with red. His hair hung black and lank under his wildcat muff hat. In the animal's eyes were water-polished glassed stones.

Ten feet away Bradley smelled him; it wasn't a bad smell. It was different. Bradley slipped just a bit on a mossy rock and the Indian held out his hand. Bradley took it and held on. They locked eyes and nodded to each other. Neither smiled or spoke for more than a minute. Bradley threw up his hand and on Perry's command all the men behind him set down their rifles to watch. He had a bone pierced through the cartilage at the bottom of his nose. When they unclasped hands he waved the other toward the field of aspen and bowed his head again. Bradley nodded. He thought he understood what he meant.

We now go, the Indian said like he'd been rehearsing this on the entire long walk down the butte and across the field to the river. A line of Indians walked out of the trees. Suddenly they were just there. They formed a straight line across maybe fifty yards from the riverside. All quiet.

It was like even the water flowing over Bradley's boots had stopped. The Indian made sounds but no words that Bradley could get. He pointed at the line of braves behind him and made the sweep motion with his arm once more. When the arm stopped he was pointing off into the distance. That was when he pulled the note from his sleeve. It was the blank on the back of a page pulled out of a soldier's manual. He handed it to Bradley and waited for him to read it over.

There were the Sioux symbols for Sitting Bull and something like English trying to say Canada. Someone had drawn a map that pointed to the north.

Leave please us alone, were the four words he could make out the most clear.

When Bradley looked up, something very strange happened. The Indian brave winked at him.

When Bradley looked back, standing there in the water with the note clutched in his hand, the Indian winked again. They shook hands, no smiles, Bradley had said not a word in the exchange. The Indian turned and walked back to the other side. Bradley stood in the water for a moment to watch and then he too turned to walk back to his men.

Huebner and Baker found Gibbon's army on the river trail and by the sixth day they made it back to the survivor camp. The Indians had rode off a couple days before, just up and left along the river north right before their eyes. Perry gave the order to save ammunition so all the soldiers did was to watch them go. When Gibbon's army came they ate a hot meal and then in twos and threes at first then by company they put hankies over their mouths and recrossed the river to bury their dead. Gibbon pulled Bradley aside and walked him back along the river.

I hear you had a meeting with them.

That's right.

Who was it?

B'lieve it was one of the Chief's sons.

Just you and him.

That's all it was. They could have come across and killed us all.

What'd he say?

Not much. He had a note they'd written out. He said they hadn't wanted to fight, but they would.

Where they going?

Ta-tanka I-yo-take.

What's that?

Sorry sir, that's the Sioux for Sitting Bull. They are trying to go to Canada. They'll only fight if we bring it to them. They'd rather just go.

Headed to Canady-i-o?

That's what it said.

They wrote it in English?

Best they could.

Bradley handed it over. Gibbon took off his hat, wiped his hand over his thinning hair, running his fingers through the places on the side that had been matted down.

Gibbon and Bradley exchanged glances. The Lieutenant hitched up his pants, then knelt down to wash his hanky off in the cold water. He used it to wipe off his face.

Sure's hot, he said.

Going to git worse, Gibbon said, and sat his haunches.

General Howard wants those Nez Perce. They were peaceable but they ain't no more. Gen'l Howard has put out word that all available armies are to go after them.

We're ready when you are, Colonel.

I know you are, James. What happened out here?

You talked to Huebner.

Course I did.

We jes walked right into it.

Was it Perry's fault?

It wasn't no one's fault. Hell, blame me if you want.

I ain't looking to blame no one. Just need to know what I got to work with. Perry lost half his men. Is he OK?

Best as can be expected, I guess.

They shouldn't have sent y'all off all hellfire like that.

They had to send someone.

Guess so. James, I got some news for you. I sent my Mary over to your Sioux.

Colonel?

She's with child, James.

You sure?

Goddamn, son, smile or something.

Hunh . . .

Mary took it upon herself to take care.

I appreciate what you done, sir.

It's jes Christian kindness is what it is. You'll have to decide what to do when you git back.

Bradley kicked at the dirt. A couple black birds lighted off the ground into the air. He watched them till they were lost in the clouds.

He found Huebner under a tree, taking a nap.

You there, son?

Hey, Cap'n.

They found Gentle.

He's here?

No, he's in Nebraska.

What did you say to Colonel Gibbon?

About what?

Huebner looked at him. He went there after that Crazy Horse.

There's nothing we can do anyway, Gus.

Doesn't really matter to me either way, just an Indian.

Ain't you gotten hard?

Maybe. These are strange times, hunh, Cap'n.

Bradley just sighed and put out his hand. Huebner took it and pulled Bradley close to him.

What about this Baker? Bradley asked.

He sure can talk all right. We going out?

That we are. And it seems that we need a man.

I guess the third one's always wild.

11

In the mountains there was a breeze, not hot and dry like out on the high plains, but with a cool feel in the day that rustled through the leaves of the trees, through the needles of the pines near their heads then turned cold when they camped at night. Bradley rode in the lead with Huebner second and Baker bringing up the rear. The trail was not hard to follow. The Indians stuck to the old way through the mountains, anything else would have been impossible close passes, sheer drops and dark passages through tall, dense ancient stands of spruce, juniper and pine.

There's no way we can keep up with these Indians, Cap'n, Baker said, and sat his horse. Not the way they know this old trail.

We'll just follow them until they stop somewhere. Then we'll get them.

What if they don't?

Oh, they will, right Gus?

Whatever you say, Cap'n.

Every night Baker talked about dying, heaven and his problem with God. Most of the time Bradley and Huebner were respectful. At least the fellow was entertaining. Once in a while they couldn't help but bait him a little. Usually Huebner started it.

What's this God's face supposed to look like?

I am waiting to see.

You mean you don't know what you're looking for? How you going to know it when you see it?

Oh, I'll know. You know when it's time to kiss a girl don't you.

Baker always seemed to get the joke himself: he had an odd little smile. But he was earnest too, you couldn't hold the silliness against him.

They camped in the culverts and leaf-filled ditches, or on the highland plateaus of deep green moss, softer than any bed of feathers they'd ever had back home. They rode the rises during the day. Bradley kept a strong pace as always. The minute he awoke in the morning he'd be walking around, restless, waiting for the others. He'd eat what breakfast there was on the mount and after a cup of coffee he was ready to ride. It was Huebner who first saw the smoke. They'd been on the trail for over a week.

Looky there, on the next rise.

I see it.

How you want to do it, Cap'n?

Before they left Gibbon had told them the army would follow down on the level ground.

They should be no more than a day or two behind us.

I could ride back.

Naw, let's ride up and take a look.

Huebner waved Bradley to the side.

You ready for this, bud?

Say what?

Just thought I'd ask. I could ride over alone to look things over.

I appreciate the thought. But I'm going too, Gus. I want to get this over and go home.

You think it's ever going to be over?

It's got to.

It ain't.

Want to flip for it?

They turned around. Hey, Baker, what's the matter?

Just thought I'd pray, sir.

Let me know when you're ready.

Sorry, sir.

All right, let's walk the horses.

We'll just have a little look-a-see, right, Cap'n?

You ain't skeered is ya, Baker?

Give him a break, Gus.

And get us killed. That's one thing Gentle was good fer.

Baker, Bradley said. Look we're all scared.

Really?

Hell yes. It don't never stop.

What they found after a careful hour walking the trail was not an Indian camp, but the dugout of an old woman. She surprised them, shooting off over their heads and covering them with a shotgun until they showed their hands.

What y'all want?

She had a greasy skin over her shoulders like a shawl with eyes bright blue, one kept flinching closed, a nervous tic.

She looks every bit of sixty, Cap'n, Baker said.

You can speak directly to me.

We're the army, mam, Bradley said.

So?

Well, you can put that gun down.

Seems like a good reason to keep it up.

They laughed.

Naw really, mam, we're on the same side here.

Don't talk to me like I'm stupid. Friend and foe. Ain't no distinction out here. What you want?

Well, have you seen any Indians?

Maybe I have, maybe I have not. I ain't going to help ya kill em. If that's what you want.

We're here to protect American citizens like yourself.

When I need it I'll ask for it. She spat. Protect me, bunch of cheeky-faced young boys like y'all.

Mam, Huebner spoke up and smiled. Why don't we all just sit down for a while?

I could use a sit. You're a tall one aren't you. And handsome too. C'mon over. Lemme get you fellows a drink. Why don't the rest of you two just be polite like this one here.

She took Huebner's arm and all Bradley and Baker could do was smile. She dug out an old green bottle from the folds of her clothes.

You ain't got a smoke somewhere do you?

Sure do, mam.

Real tobacco?

Nature's best.

Mary Jesus. Let's all sit down then.

She led them to a felled tree that looked down over a wandering stream far below. Her liquor made them laugh and their eyes water when they swallowed.

You boys just ought to go back, she said.

Mam? Bradley said.

You can't just come here and take it away. Army men or not.

Mam?

You'll suffer for it. You're bound to.

We already have, Bradley said.

Hmm, I guess that's so.

How do you know this? Baker asked

What do you mean how do I know? They been here forever. They came with the land, just like the trees, just like the grubs and the slugs.

How long you been here, mam? Bradley asked.

Mercy, I fell off a wagon train. They thought I was crazy, Crazy Woman Walking that's the name of this place. I'm on the map I am.

That must have been over ten or twelve years ago. I heard that story, Bradley said.

Mercy Mary, son. Did I make it up? What do I have to lie about?

To Bradley she said, I didn't want to tell you this. You look like my brother.

All right, mam.

They just left me out here to die. But I didn't.

I'm sure they didn't mean for it to come out like that, Bradley said.

Really you think?

Yes, mam. They must have looked for you.

You think so?

Of course I do.

You're a sweet boy. You are all three sweet boys. Why don't you just go on home?

We're the army, Baker said.

Hmm, I guess so. Let me tell you something about these Indians.

You leave them alone, they'll sure leave you alone. They aren't like the others.

Wish it were that easy, mam.

It's not then.

No, mam, it's not.

Hmm.

You been out here for ten years.

Guess so.

You ever want to go back, maybe we could take you back, Baker said.

Ain't you sweet. Maybe next time. Check with me next time. You are all three sweet boys. Why don't all of you go home?

What if that woman wasn't there at all?

It was Baker talking, the campfire was down to coals. In the dark the distant mountains were clear blue, with the sky misted with rain from gray puffs of cloud directly over their heads. They rode down through a tall meadow green grass plateau and up the next rise where they made camp.

What are you talking about, soldier?

I don't know, just thinking.

Don't we get the winners, Cap'n?

Let him talk, Gus.

I don't know, it just seems so unreal.

What do you mean? Bradley asked.

We're out in the Crazy Woman Mountains and we see this smoke, and then there's a woman, a white woman all alone. It's like a children's story. Like we dreamed it up.

So.

Says she's been there for a decade, ran off from a wagon train, hiding in the mountains all alone by herself for all that time.

Well anyone could be a little crazy, Bradley said. We don't have to believe her.

I ain't talking about all that.

I still got no idea what you are talking about, Huebner said.

Here it is, Gus. Let's say I'm dreaming.

All right, that's easy enough to imagine.

C'mon, Gus, Bradley said.

I'm just kidding the boy.

It's all right. I don't mind, Baker said, and gave him his half-smile. I could dream, sure, but I don't think all of us could. Do you think that's possible?

We all saw her though. We can't all dream the same thing.

How do you know?

It's times like this makes a man miss old Billy Gentle, Huebner said.

Go ahead, Baker, Bradley said. Don't mind him.

I don't, Baker said. We're out here in this place. It's awful and it's beautiful. We ain't never been here before.

But we sat down with her, Huebner said. She gave us the strange liquor.

He ain't denying any of that, Bradley said. He's just saying. Hell, Baker, what are you saying?

I get it, Cap'n, Huebner laughed. This is one of those Pennsyltuckee things. Never ride with someone who don't know even the name of their own state.

Hah, hah, hah, very funny, Mr. Gus from New Jersey. Baker laughed out loud. Sure, we saw her, she was there. But it was as much like a dream as anything else.

Are you saying we made it happen, Bradley asked, by thinking it, by wanting it?

We weren't thinking of it, Huebner said. Hell I wasn't.

Maybe, Cap'n. Baker ignored Huebner. I just like to wonder about things.

That's the way it is out here, Bradley said.

Say what, Cap'n?

I kind of see what he's saying.

How do we know what's what?

Out here?

Hell ever, Baker said. He got to his feet and started pacing around the fire. We take all this stuff for granted, the sky, the color of night. How do we know? I have to see something.

But she was there, Huebner insisted.

Sure she was. Of course she was. What about that Indian, Cap'n—the one you met out in the water?

C'mon, Baker, that happened. All of this has happened. I can't half-tell you the damn things I seen. There ain't no words for it all.

That's it then. Baker was excited and waving his arms. Now he came to a stop.

It was kind of like a dream, Bradley said. That whole thing with the Indian, sometimes I still believe it happened.

Burying those poor fellows out there in the field. After they all been dead for days. You can put it into words, but that don't make it what happened.

It's called staying sane, Bradley said.

Back east the preachers and the paper-writers put it all into words, but that's all it is. We got to carry the real thing around with us. Someday we're all going to have to go back to the world, those of us that live. Who's going to believe us?

Probably best to say nothing about it at all, Huebner said, serious now. A flaming log fell off the fire. He kicked it back in and took a drink from his canteen.

I don't know. I don't know if I could do that.

You might have to try, Bradley said.

I'm just saying what if. You can't fault a guy for saying what if.

You're going to a hard place, Baker, Bradley said.

You think?

I been there.

12

He didn't have a plan. Gentle rode down over wide open grassland steppes, folding into one another, land shelf shifts marked only by grass and shaley chips of stone, long meadows and enormous blue skies. He wasn't even sure where he was going, or that he couldn't go back. He had no food with him. When he was caught in a three-day squall on the low mountain plains, he kept riding. He stopped only for his horse to drink from the rapids of the rivers, the Bighorn, the Cottonwood and the Rosebud. When the sky cleared, he slept on his horse in the long hot afternoons when the heat shimmered in the air, and turned his eyes to sharp cuts in his face. When he slit his eyes like that the ground turned into a thousand glittering diamonds. He thought he might go home and cried on his horse, kicked the tears away in the breeze that galloped past when he saw all at once this was it. He rode through untamed deep forestlands, over lush green mountainsides, aboriginal, volcanic grassed highlands, red rock clay, big fog-shrouded meadowlands. He wasn't afraid of dying.

He felt a little sentimental and lonely, took the way past the battlefields of the last year. He found a U.S. button. He saw rattlesnakes, crickets, bees, purple sweet pink puff plants, clover, dandelions, toads, a swamp with black algae, cat-tails, grass poking from the red sand dirt of a draw down to the water, blue lupine and yellow lilies, cracks in the earth, fallen dead trees, blue dragonflies and field mice. He camped in the ravine where he'd been shot in the leg and built a fire over the bones he found from dead Sioux. He talked to his horse and told it stories.

Gentle rode onto the grounds of Fort Robinson in the purple dark of night. Here in Nebraska Territory the field was still wide open, no gate or guards just a wide open bowl with the hills leading to the distant box buttes. He rode slowly across the silent parade grounds, sat his horse for a minute to listen to it pull at the grass with its bared teeth. There was a candle glowing from the window of the office in the command house. It was a squat building maybe ten feet high, fifteen feet deep, made out of logs with mud and grass and mortar stuck in the cracks. When he walked over to look through the cut square hole, he saw the General named Crook staring off into the nothing beyond the candle's glow with a bottle and a tin coffee cup beside him on the table. When Gentle next walked over to peer in the other hole he saw something stand up, chained to the wall. Just moonlight. He thought he saw eyes. He wondered if it was the one he came for.

Crook saw him standing in the doorway and called to him.

C'mon in, son, ain't it windy out there. The wind is strange out here innit?

Yes, sir.

You ain't cold is you?

No, sir.

C'mon in here and have a drink. I just made coffee. Or ya ken crack that bottle there. Never touch the stuff m'self.

The General looked to the window. Y'know sometimes I listen to the wind and I almost hear a song, he said.

There ain't enough music out here.

That's right, son, Crook said. He offered the bottle and Gentle took a drink.

Thanks, he said.

Where you been, son? I know you, don't I?

We met a long time ago. We met with Reno.

Ahh, right, the Bradley boy. Reno. They just put him on trial, y'know.

For what?

For going and getting all his boys killed.

They can do that?

Hell, son, they can do whatever they want. Don't you go and forgit that. Not ever. They broke that man.

They gonna kill him?

Might as well, son. They didn't take his stripes or nothing, but they broke that man.

The wind howled and Crook shivered. He had a knife he was sharpening on a stone. He put out his finger and poked the end until the knife drew blood, licked off the blade then washed it down with a hit from the tin cup.

You bring your boys with you?

I came alone.

You did now. What fer?

Gentle cast his eyes toward the dark doorway at the back of the room. The moon came in from the other side and cast a shadowed glow from the darkness space.

Oh yeah we got us a live one in there. Mister Horse hisself. Hey CrazyHead, Crook hollered.

I like to sit here, just me and him, we's the ones who can't sleep.

That's why I come.

That so.

Seems like it's why we're all out here ain't it. Might as well see it all the way through. Don't you think, General?

You're a bold boy. How old are you, son?

I don't see as how that matters t'all, sir.

Did I say it did? Man can ask a question can't he?

Guess so. Past eighteen I guess. We never were much for counting where I come from.

Here, have another drink. Whose command are you under? You weren't always with Bradley were ya?

You the General, sir.

Son, don't backtalk me now, I could break this bottle over your head and feed you to the dogs out yonder. No one would ask a single question about it either.

No one's denying that, sir. Wouldn't be right, though.

I left right behind a long time ago, son.

The General looked sad. The shadows were long on his face and he looked old.

What we going to do with the Indian, sir? If you don't mind my asking.

Crook swallowed and looked Gentle over. I offered him a place in the army, to go and chase the Nez Perce. I b'lieve he could make a good soldier.

Really, like them Crows?

Don't look at me like that, son. Some of his boys already done joined up. But not this one, but not this one. Can't say I blame him. Can't say I don't admire him.

He's just an Indian, sir.

That he is, son. We're going to put him on a train and send him down to Florida. We got a special place for ones like him. Crook took a draw from his pipe, looking toward the dark doorway. Then he laughed of a sudden.

C'mon let's take a look at him. Ready for the carnival, son? You come all this way. Y'ever been to the zoo? It's open, now.

Crook lurched to his feet. Bring the candle, I'll bring the bottle.

The moonlight showed his form, his arms thrust out to both sides and shackled to the wall. His long, brown hair hung down and covered his face.

Take a good whiff, son. That there's the hoss-man. The Crazy one hisself. That there's one rank Indian.

The Indian raised his head and looked at each of them, for a second, then let his hair fall down.

He ain't much for respecting his superiors. Had to chain him up since he run off a couple a days ago. G'wan, son, put that candle up closer to his face. Let's us have a look at the old hoss-man.

Gentle did as he was told.

G'wan keep going. He likes fire this one. He's a warrior king. Put it right up to his chin, boy. I thought that's why you come here.

Gentle brought the flame so it singed the brown hair, a strange smell. When he raised his head, his eyes were black and the flame glittered off of them.

What you scared of, boy? He likes this kind of thing. He's trained for it. That old boy done walked through fire.

Gentle held the candle so the flame barely touched the point of the Indian's chin.

He didn't draw back. All at once he opened his mouth and bit off the flame and the tip of the candle then spit it back at Gentle.

Gentle jumped back, he couldn't help it.

Haw Marie! That's one Crazy Indian. Ain't he a beauty, son? Ain't he? Here, let's give the old hoss-man a drink.

Gentle took the bottle himself.

Here wild-man, open up.

He put the bottle against the Indian's lip, jammed up against his teeth.

You ain't thirsty is you?

C'mon, son, let's go and finish that up. He ain't a going nowhere. You'll have your chance.

I hope you got another cup, sir.

Say what?

Cos I ain't drinking after no Indian.

Lemme light the candle. Crook laughed. Sure let me just get you a cup. Sure, son.

They talked into the night. Gentle finished the bottle and Crook let Gentle roll himself up some tobacco. By morning the prisoner had a new guard.

— 13 —

The scouts skirted straight down the mountains, sidestepping the horses through a cut in the great Bitterroot Range. Gibbon and the troops had stayed out of the mountains and rode along the other way. They met them in a meadow coming up on the camp in the late afternoon as the sun set red under a slowly pulled blue curtain of sky. They found Gibbon by a fire toward the edge of the camp, the field dotted with clumps of men shouting, shooting off their guns. Some of them even had harmonicas out. Everybody was drinking.

Evenin', Lieutenant Bradley. Gibbon stumbled and took Bradley's hand as much to steady himself as for greeting. His face flushed and he took off his hat and wiped his brow. Excuse me, son, he said slowly, formally. Gibbon was as drunk as Bradley had ever seen him.

Evening, Colonel, Bradley said. You remember Huebner and Baker.

Gibbon looked their way. Outfit your men with some food and drink, then join me by the fire, Lieutenant.

Yes, sir.

Gibbon got up to go to the pot and stumbled into the fire, stood there in the middle of it until his boots steamed and smoke curled up around his pants.

Bradley looked at his scouts, who had taken a step back. He nodded them away and went to the Colonel's side. Huebner and Baker sidled up to another group of men, while Bradley joined Gibbon.

I can get mine, sir, he said.

Gibbon frowned, brushed ashes off his boots and sat down heavily. You'll have to excuse me, Lieutenant. Colonel's a little drunk tonight.

Is Cap'n Perry here, sir?

Gibbon yanked his thumb at a dark form under two or three blankets.

He's already had his, Gibbon said and sighed deeply. He took a drink from his tin cup. I been picking up new recruits on the way up, Gibbon said. We been pushing hard and the morale's been kind a low. Y'all find any of those hostiles?

We followed a pretty strong trail, for a while, then lost it again in the mountains. Then we saw more fires and it was y'all.

Gibbon nodded, drinking while Bradley ate. Well, you're headed in the right direction, the Colonel said. We got strong reports of where they's at.

Is that so? How close are they?

That's the thing, James. The Colonel lowered his head and spat. He looked around. Where's old Blackie? Black, he hollered out and a man maybe ten feet away came forward out of the gathering darkness.

You remember Mr. Black, don't you, James.

Of course, Bradley said, and rose to shake the man's hand. I'd thought you'd gone on after that mess up there in the hill.

Evening, Cap'n. I rode fer a week. I went all the way to Stevensville to spend the night. I walked into the supply store and there they were. By my father's grave, I swear I was sober, the man called Black went on. There they were the Ned Percys themselves.

In Stevensville?

Gibbon cleared his throat loudly, but did not speak.

They raided the town?

They did not. Them reds paid in gold. They traded fair and square for everything they took.

The Indians did?

Not all of them are hostile, Gibbon broke in. They been living with the white folks out here for a while now, Lieutenant.

I say they did, over my mama's grave. Didn't even git drunk. Chief told them to lock up all the likker. Them Ned Percys are a breed unto themselves.

They all are, Bradley said.

True words, sir. The one called Black shook his head and the three of them were silent for a moment. The fire before them shifted, a log fell down into the red cinders and sparks rose and faded into the misty smoke toward the sky.

When was this? Bradley asked.

Couple days ago is all. I was feeling antsy about leaving y'all and after that I just had to ride back and find yas.

Old Blackie was with the regiment that shot down old Stonewall back in the war, Gibbon said.

I had my fill of it, Colonel, if that's what you mean. That there Jackson was a great man. Hell I don't care which side you were on. It took my heart to see him die like that the way he done.

Black reached for the bottle then beside Gibbon's boot.

You know where they are? Bradley asked.

Black threw his arm back behind him. I believe they should be just beyond those hills right there.

What are your orders, Colonel? If I may say I would be honored to lead a party to meet with them.

No, son. Tomorrow morning, we attack.

Yes, sir. Bradley swallowed, scraping off his plate with a wedge of hardtack.

When you're ready I'd like for you to take your boys to have a look, James.

I'm ready now, sir.

I don't know how good I feel about having old Perry here leading any more charges.

Sir?

I want you to lead them in. You and your boys.

I ain't their Cap'n though.

Hell, James, the whole damn army knows about y'all and your boys.

Bradley took a drink. With the Colonel's permission I'd like to have a look at their position. I can get my men and . . .

Don't bother them, son. Take Black here with you. He can show y'all where they are. Through those woods there's a cliff looking down on a long draw. You can see their camp plain as day from there.

All right then, sir.

Bradley and Black left Gibbon staring into the fire. They found the other scouts and Bradley told them the news.

You don't want us to go with you now, Cap'n? Huebner asked then.

Y'all finish your dinner, Gus. If we're not back in a half-hour, you can worry. Colonel says we fight in the morning. Huebner nodded, then sat down again with Baker by their fire. Quietly the two of them watched Bradley and Black set out across the meadow afoot.

In the dark there was a bald eagle they saw against the sky, swoop down the face of a rocky steppe and disappear behind a pale brown mountain, after something. Baker and Huebner were still by the fire.

See that.

And what would that be, Reverent Baker?

The eagle, Baker said, and accepted a flask from Huebner. You shouldn't call me that, he said quietly.

I was just kidding, son.

You ain't got no right to call me that. Ain't nothing to make no fun about, that.

What do you want to know, Baker? You want to know about God?

Naw, Gus, I'm sorry.

Did I think about God when I shot a bunch of poor horses? When I had to kill or die m'self. That what you want to know? Did I see God. You want to know did I see his face?

Gus.

Damnit, Baker. Didn't anyone ever tell you nothing? You can't ask a man about something like that. Din't ya ever think about that?

Not really. Some of the stories I heard about what the Indians done to Custer's boys and such. I said well they ain't Christians. But we're white men. We got God for us.

I wouldn't be so sure.

C'mon.

No you c'mon.

I ain't, I din't mean to.

Naw it's all right. Anything left in that bottle?

Corporal August Huebner took a long drink and tried to speak while the liquor still burned in his throat.

You don't know where you are yet do you?

What? What do you mean?

You'll see.

What are you talking about?

Ain't nothing to be told. You don't know who you are yet.

Andrew George Baker.

Shit. I ain't never talked so much about it. If you been out there you know better I guess. I can't expect that out of you.

What do you mean?

It ain't got nothing to do with God. Let's just leave God out of it.

All right.

I don't know. They're trying to kill you, and you them. Something just comes out of you. I seen men run, heard them calling out for their mamas. I seen men talking every crazy thing. I seen men . . .

What? Seen what?

Seen men do things I could never imagine.

Baker just looked at Huebner and was silent.

I done em. I done a lot of other things. Maybe tomorrow I'll do some more.

Huebner looked away.

Mebbe, Baker said.

Mebbe, you get scared of what you see, so you keep going because you git scared. Maybe some just enjoy. Indians are just dogs anyway, they say. It's like when you try something you never thought you would and you like it. You hate that you've done it, but you like how it feels. Or you can't believe you're doing it so you do it harder. And God, he just stands by and watches.

14

All day, every day the Indians came by the jail. Gentle only let them in one at a time and sometimes in twos and threes. Everyone that came brought something for the Oglala chief. They laid the bones, amulets, pouches, even moccasins at his feet, said prayers and then made way for the next person. They brought teeth, human and animal, elaborate skins and blankets, a child's boot, inlaid pipes and the insides of animals, from buffalo, horses, to wildcats, antelopes. At first Gentle checked everything they brought in, after a while he just said to hell with it. His partner, a kid name of Hamilton from Maryland by way of Scotland, picked out the things he liked and told his plan to sell them later to the soldiers.

No one's going to want that stuff.

Say what?

Bad religion, son. Sides you can get that for half a nothing, for a goddamn sip of whiskey, from any of the settlers all around here and in the hills.

You think you a-right?

Sure I'm right.

Hamilton was the skinniest man Gentle had ever seen. His cheeks sunken, his eyes dark and red holes. His face was all nose. He had a hung back and smelled rank. He took a look down the long line, rubbed his nose and spat.

How long they been coming in like this? Gentle asked.

Ever since they brought him back in the other day.

What happened?

Hamilton took a drink from his flask and offered it to Gentle, who declined. The sun had barely risen over the buttes on a chilly raw gray day. It couldn't be past nine o'clock in the morning. He wanted some coffee. He was waiting for Crook to finish his morning meetings so he could slip into the command post and get him some.

Oh, Hamilton said. They had him in the barracks down yonder where they brought them all when they first come in.

Were there guards?

Not really.

This is crazy. It's been the same since I come.

Yeah boy, I believe something's going to have to give.

Gentle told Hamilton stories from his days in the field, to everything he said the Scot just squinted his bloodshot eyes and said huh or ain't that something.

You ain't that bright is ya?

That's what everone's always said. Ma said it was cos she dropped me on my head when I was little. She always felt bad about that.

'Sat right.

When Gentle went in to see Crook, the General said, Howdy. Quite a little freak show we got here, eh, son?

Sorriest bunch I ever seen.

Yeah, we're going to have to cut this thing off. It ain't no good.

Why do you let them come on like this?

I don't know. Some of the other officers are worried about trouble.

I don't see how with him all chained up.

That's my thinking, son. Do the Indians some good to see that boy all chained up like that. If I could get ever single Indian in the country to come by I would.

The others could start something.

Yeah they could.

Crook looked out of the hole in the wall, pulling one of his beard-braids down, twisting the greasy end with his fingers.

Son, there's something we got to settle out.

What would that be, sir?

Did Gibbon send y'all out here?

What you mean?

Don't play possum with me, son. I asked you a straight question.

There wasn't nothing happening out there. I went for rides all the time.

How long it take you to get here?

I don't know, mebbe a week, mebbe more.

Goddamn, son. You can't just be running off around like that.

Sir?

Yore in the army. As long as you got the uniform on, you got to follow orders. You could get shot for what you done.

Sir.

You know that.

Aww, c'mon, sir.

We got to give you a hearing, son.

What's that?

Damn it to hell. We got to get testimony. I got to get word to Gibbon and Bradley, see what they want to do with ya.

You going to hang me?

We might have to. From the highest damn tree we can find. Maybe we'll stick you in with that crazy Indian for a few days.

Excuse me sir, but goddamn. That Indian's our'n. We're the ones that went all the way out to hell and back to find em.

Did you bring him in?

Hell, sir, we shoulda.

Son, listen at me here. I like you. Been watching you. I seen what you done with Bradley in the American Horse thing and with MacKenzie with the Cheyenne. But if Gibbon wants to raise a stink, he can.

You ain't gone to shoot me?

Damn you are a young one, ain't ya?

Old enough to do all I done.

Damn, well, you got your orders for now.

Sir, this ain't right. I ain't the enemy.

Don't raise your voice to me, son. So long as you're here I can keep an eye on ya. You run off anywheres we'll have to shoot you.

There was a sharp crack, and loud voices.

Hey, what the hell was that? Ahh shit, c'mon, son.

Gentle was already out the door. The parade ground was in chaos when they got out there. Hamilton was flat on his back, moaning with his face bleeding and a knife sticking out his belly.

They all came at once, Billy boy.

Hamilton grit his teeth and then pulled the knife out.

They all come at once, he said.

They broke him out, another soldier spoke up.

Corporal Gentle grabbed his rifle. He saw the one called Crazy Horse in a crowd, swarming and hollering. He had a bayonet in each of his hands. He waved them in the air, threatening the soldiers.

There were a lot of other Indians around. One came up behind Crazy Horse and grabbed him from behind. There was a struggle.

That's when Gentle ran into the melee. He went down to his knees a couple of times, trying to get a clean shot off. There were too many other people. He would remember later he had his bayonet drawn. He got within a couple feet of the Indian when the crowd suddenly surged. He caught him in the back, right under the left ribcage. Suddenly his bayonet was shiny with blood and the Oglala Chief called Crazy Horse was lying in the dirt. A line of soldiers had come up. They shot into the air and the rest of the Indians scattered. For a long moment it was just Gentle and the bleeding Indian lying beside him in the dirt. Gentle could see his ribs rise and fall ever so slightly.

Gentle saw Crook and a tall man with black sideburns, some others. He heard someone call out for a Doc, sideburns answered. When Gentle got up and walked away, no one moved to stop him.

15

The birds darted and swooped among the falling leaves and rode in the wind. They moved in and out of the breeze more graceful for the leaves falling, chattering at the yellow sunlight that slanted down through the tops of the trees. Hawks on the trees high up, looking down to the verdant islands in the blue, low lying water gulley, there beyond the wide sagebrush valley rimmed with the pines, pale blue peaks in the distant west, black chipmunks with long tails and big robins pecking the black dirt after worms. Bradley was surprised when he awoke. He hadn't known he'd slept. Must have been the liquor. He suspected he was still a little drunk. After speaking with Gibbon and the others, he and Black had walked across a long field of tall grass toward the raw mud butte. They skirted the edge into a deep pine-woods that came out on a hill overlooking a long draw down into a river cut valley. Here's where they saw the smoke from the Nez Perce's campfires. Black just put his nose in the wind and pointed to the edge of the trees. He made a motion with his hands down to indicate the long sloped drop down the hill. Bradley nodded. He wanted a better look. There was pine with low branches and heavy cover. He got a boost from Black's clasped hands and hoisting himself up, hand over hand, he climbed the pine tree to get a better look. In the moonlight the water below had glowed silver. The draw down to the valley went for one hundred yards into a dense thicket of willows around a marshy section of the river. The Indians were camped on the long flat bed of the valley beyond the trees, the slanted draw and the marsh.

If we get the men here tonight, we can go down before dawn.

That's it.

Let's tell the Colonel.

Gibbon didn't bother to get the men into formation. After Bradley and Black came back the word passed through camp and the men started to ride and walk in the direction of the Indian campsite. They shared what liquor was left on the way over and within two hours they'd massed at the edge of the woods. Down below the village of maybe seventy teepees was quiet. They had to run down the hill to attack.

Gibbon sent Bradley with his men to one end and he stayed at the other. When he gave the signal they all went down the hill and tried to take it from both ends. Huebner and Baker had the fastest horses and were the first ones in the camp. It was quiet, Baker could see the dew glinting off the grass, still blue from the last of the dark. They trampled over the teepees with their horses, clubbing the dark forms that came awake. There was an old man behind a stump, fallen asleep on the watch. Bradley looked right into his eyes when they opened. There was a moment of recognition. He made to rise. His throat made a dry, clicking sound. Huebner shot him and he sat back down, looking at the red hole in his bare belly. Colonel Gibbon's infantry soldiers ran through the encampment in a wave, stopping in lines to strafe the village, then tearing into the clearing, pulling the teepees off the sleeping families.

Private Andrew George Baker's gun jammed and he cussed it, using it as a club. His first kill was a brave. Huebner had pulled down the tent. The man held his child, looked up with the baby curled by his chest. Baker just reared back and smacked him across the face. He remembered the sound of the metal on bone: the man bit down on his tongue and a piece just flew off. Baker could see the stream of blood and spit. He pulled up his horse. When he tried his gun again, it jerked against his shoulder, a puff of smoke curled in his nostrils and the man's neck opened up red. By now his wife and babes were screaming, wide-mouthed. Baker could see the tears running down their faces when they were shot. It all took maybe ten seconds then he was a different man. All three of the scouts were able to make it to the woods at the end of the camp. They mounted a trail halfway up the rise just beyond the line of trees.

They had set their horses and stopped off to have a quick drink. Through the pines the first morning rays of the sun glinted off the marsh water. Indians and soldiers splashed into the water hand to hand. When they heard noises in the woods just below, Bradley held up his hand quiet, tied his horse quickly to a branch.

Bradley went forward maybe five steps from the others to see what it was. Huebner and Baker both saw the brave step out of the green. There was a flash, Bradley's head snapped back and then he was on the ground and Indians swarmed all over them. One came out from behind every tree. Huebner felt a blow like a hammer to his chest. All at once they were gone and everyone was lying on their backs. He was next to Bradley looking at his ruined head. He knew he was dead.

When the Indians were gone, Huebner got up and started walking. His head was ringing and he couldn't breathe too well. The sun came down through the trees and dappled the pine straw on the ground. He saw something silver glinting in his hand. When he opened it there was a little piece of tin.

J. H. Bradley.

It was a little collar clasp. Huebner saw the flash in his head again. The memory was the color of blood, the sound of the shot, the spray that hit him in the face and made him blink his eyes. At the time it did not register that it was the Captain's blood that hit him, his blood and his brain.

When Huebner came to on the ground he saw part of the Captain's jaw, with his teeth there sticking out, lying next to his bleeding neck. The sun glinted off the piece of tin with his name on it. Huebner picked that up and started walking. He just didn't want to be there anymore. He wanted to go away. Huebner had raised his gun and shot the Nez Perce brave, three maybe four shots. Baker got him too. The Indian started walking backwards, taking another step as each blow hit him, in the chest he turned, in the chest again he stepped straight back, in the stomach he doubled over, in the shoulder shot his back straight out again. He was hit with too many bullets for him to fall over right away.

There were maybe twenty troopers there. They were overrun. Huebner saw the war club, like a rock thrown through the air as it hit him in the chest. Then he was on the ground. Something was dripping into his eyes that he had to wipe off to see. That was Bradley's blood. He felt like he couldn't breathe.

Baker yelled at him as he walked away.

Everyone's going this way. C'mon the army's this way. Where are you going?

Huebner didn't have anything at all to say.

He walked all the way out through the woods into a long, open field. Grasshoppers jumped with his every step. Faint gray crickets.

There was a slight breeze, warm. Butterflies white and yellow just floating specks of bright color set against the blue sky in the glaring sun. The sounds of the soldiers and Indians all faded away. After a while even Baker's questions had stopped. He wanted his mind to stop too. He tried to concentrate on the field. The ringing in his head was like a big bell that changed all the sounds and even what he saw. Everything hurt a little bit. A couple of horses had gotten away with him. He kept his distance, heard the sound of them pulling up grass to eat. In the distance, across the long long field there was a one stark butte face. He would walk on until he got there. He pushed through the tall grass with his boots, little specks of seed dotted the leather. Just the toe-ends were a little moist. There were piles of straw, horse dumps that looked like grass again as if they'd never even been through the horse and back out. All bleached-out and white. He stepped on a bunch of the wildflowers. He felt dizzy and his mouth was dry.

Sometimes he heard Baker's voice again. It kept getting farther away.

He felt like he wanted to sit down but then he saw the Indian dancing backwards, in slow motion with dust kicking up all around, and bullets rippling back the leaves of the tree behind him. Weeds, bug carcasses, rocks in the middle, forever changing, slow time, from fly time to rock time, rocks look like bones, bones that look like rocks or human forms like a nose sticking out. Living and dead are all together on the prairie. The orange butterflies fly always a bit ahead of walker, reptile armored grasshoppers, orange legs colored like a rainbow on a pond. Big short pickle-like husk on long thick stalks, shelf of topsoil underneath. Yellow buttercups, white butterflies, earth-colored butterflies, big gnat swarms, constant itch, giant ant hump castles of dried mud, red ants, constant bug contact and accompaniment, harassment with sun and so many creatures, some small as specks of dust, colored bright orange; an old wrinkled and scraggly tree that hums with the sound of a thousand insects, amber grass, green weeds, green grass, dead of all amongst'd, bumble bees, walk through fly swarms, vulva-shaped Queen Anne's Lace, hundreds of unnameable weeds. And yellow baby's breath, purple tipped long snout, Black-eyed Susans, wild sunflowers, underwater flora, white lily blossoms, husks of old flowers turned brown.

Baker was crying. He didn't want to stop.

All those men back there. They are all dead.

This was what he wanted to tell Huebner. Those were the words, but they came out of his mouth as breathing whimpers. Huebner just kept walking though, like he was dead too. Baker just followed after him.

When they made it to the rock face the sun had dipped in the sky so that it was behind the butte. It was cold in the shadow there. He followed where he'd seen Huebner walk up. There was a worn trail that led through clumps of grass and sharp rocks that had fallen off the mount. He climbed up round the side to the top. He could see Huebner up there now. He just sat up there, looking back to from where they'd come.

It took him awhile to get all the way to the top, and when he did the sun had all but gone down behind them. Just the ghost of day was left. Huebner sat there with his back against the only tree, a weathered pine with all its branches blown off into stubs and just a few green needles sticking out from odd places.

Huebner's legs dangled out over the edge, boots rested on a stone that jutted out from the face of the mud butte.

When he saw Baker he nodded, then after a while started talking: How you think they made these things? Huebner asked. I was just thinking and wondering. They got stones with what looks like bones sticking out of em. I'm wondering if they buried things in em. Man told me no once. I asked him. Said they were the hard places left by time after the wind blew everything else away.

Baker waited until he was finished.

You just walked away.

There's no point in running from that sort of thing, Huebner said. He swallowed and looked over the field from where they'd come. Baker wiped off his face now. He guessed it must be all right to do that, now that Huebner was here, that he'd stopped and he wasn't all alone out there anymore.

I brought yore gun for you, Baker said.

Both of the soldiers were exhausted and they dropped off to sleep where they sat, there on the edge of the butte that night. In the morning when they awoke they were surrounded.

The Indians let them live. Baker and Huebner had to walk until dark. They followed the old trails of the buffalo, rolling rounded golden grasslands into buttes, rocky cliffs over riverwater, hot blue skies, a few pale clouds, yellow sprig wildflowers, bright yellow pale and purple wildflowers, occasional deer, white butterflies, golden husked grass. The Nez Perce tied them by their outstretched wrists and their necks, each to a horse. They had to walk behind. Huebner didn't want to fall; he had to move in a funny way, keeping his neck free. He figured he'd die if he fell, of a broken neck, or worse, be strangled. The rope was hairy and it burned. Mostly his horse walked, but once in a while it would gallop and Huebner would have to run along behind.

Easy now, Baker called to his horse. There was no rider. The horse was just as scared as he was.

It was really one hell of a thing to do to a man. Huebner could hardly think, lest he lose his footing and fall over. It felt like drowning all the time. His wrists were separated, pulled out maybe a foot wider than the width of his body. The horse had a cross of sticks lashed to its back with ropes bound tight to that. The poor spooked horse kept trying to shake out of it, walking sideways, once or twice backwards before it settled down.

Baker felt sorry for his horse. Once it bent down almost to its knees, then it bucked and ran. Baker fell down. He just hollered and was dragged.

Huebner thought for sure his buddy was a goner, but the boy kept grunting and hollering. Huebner couldn't turn his head to watch. He just saw the horse take off and the cloud of dust that kicked off of Baker. Then his horse took off after them.

Baker started laughing. He just let go. He couldn't get to his feet. There was no way to do it. He just had to wait. It was like he wasn't there anymore. Like he climbed up out of his body and was watching himself from the horse or from the wings of the birds that followed them. The birds swooped down so low he thought he could hear their wings. When the horse stopped, it shook itself with a spasmodic jerk, like it was wet and trying to shake off all the water. Baker got to his feet and tried his best to spit the dirt out of his mouth, but all he tasted was the dry, grit, sandy earth and blood. He couldn't swallow and breathing was hard. His tongue was in the way; he felt it getting bigger in his mouth. The left side of his pants had caught and ripped. His ass burned and his leg went numb except where he could feel the stones and burrs come through his skin and sting underneath. The rope burned his wrists and rubbed his neck raw.

They rode north along the water, over a long dry rise that followed the bends of the river with the mountains on all sides. Baker got back to his feet. He looked over at Huebner. Saw how bad he was, all dust and raw scrape wounds, sunburnt, a couple of grim eyes, and knew he must look as bad. No expression at all but the recognition they were there. The wind kicked up then and it felt cool on his sweat-soaked back.

They went up the hill into lands of tall green grass. The water in the river beside them was so blue in the hot sun. Huebner tried to imagine he could taste it. Nothing else would matter after this, he heard his mind say to him, but there was no answer back. He could see the birds. He thought one of them was a hawk. The Indians stayed mostly ahead of them, the women and children on horses with the men; a few on foot. It was all sort of a blur. They skirted a butte and walked beside the river that cut right up against its steep exposed stone bank. Huebner could see the groove in the mountain, dirt worn away to sharp rock-face where the water had borne it away. The grass gave way to pine straw and then they were in the woods. Huebner finally caught up to his horse and put some slack in the rope. He was less than human, just a prisoner, an animal and it was better for now. He was tied to a horse. The Indians could kill him at any moment. Maybe they had, maybe this was what had happened. For a moment, walking along under the blinding sun, August Huebner wondered when it had happened and how. He retraced his steps after the last battle, after Bradley's head exploded. The surface of the sandy dirt shimmered. He could see each grain, and the yellowed gray shoots of dead grass, whipped back by the breeze that swept over the prairie, hot, so dry he could taste the earth's thirst for moisture through his skin. Maybe he'd gone with the Cap'n. Maybe they were leading him to hell.

For all I done.

What he whispered to himself was drowned out by the constant silvery sound call of the hoppers, that he not only heard but felt in the dried black blood in his ears. All that day he wasn't sure; he went in and out. It was a way to block out everything, to think maybe it wasn't there. When that night the stars lit one at a time through the topmost branches of the trees, they were still walking.

Baker came up beside him. He tried to talk but he could not get his tongue out of his throat.

Huebner just looked at him. He thought he might still be able to talk himself, but there wasn't anything to say. Blue darkness fell like a soft mist all around through the trees. The Indians just walked around them, dark mounds on their own horses. He missed Cap'n Bradley, he wanted to wipe his friend's blood off his face. He wondered if Gentle were still alive. He felt all soft inside that he was still alive himself. Felt a little guilty for dreaming all the day that maybe he was not. He counted his steps one after another to make sure.

Baker kept his mouth open and concentrated on the little space where he could still get air through. His nose had been filled with dirt and blocked up, but in the darkness he snorted to clear it. It was better now. The woods out here in the dark had such a pretty smell.

When they stopped finally the moon was on high, a sharp crescent in a black gray shrouded sky and its light gave the sky a pale glow. They were given water between them to share from a cup carved out of wood. The Indian that brought it to them put it to their lips. They'd been untied from the horses. Another held a gun on his lap. His eyes were closed but the dead crystals in the animal on his head glowed green in the moonlight. Huebner didn't have the will in his body to get up and make a run for it. He wasn't scared. Maybe it'd be better to be shot. It was all gone, left somewhere in the long fields behind him. When he looked at Baker he was moving his lips, all swollen, cut and bled to black.

What are they going to do to us?

Huebner just looked at him.

They wouldn't drag us all this way, Baker's breath wheezed through his throat, just to kill us.

What's stopping them?

Baker tried to run. His leg buckled under him, his feet got tangled and he fell down. It was an awful thing to see. The Indian's eyes blinked open, he raised his gun but didn't shoot. He just kneeled over him when he fell, helped him off the ground and led him back to the tree where Huebner was. Huebner bowed his head and tried to get his lips around the piece of dried meat they'd given him to gnaw on. He could hear some of them talking. The sounds they made were not like words. For every word-sound there was a bird squawk or a whistle. They always whistled when they talked, like they had holes in their mouths that wind came through. It wasn't like it had been with the Crow. He had no idea what they were talking about. It was like they had a whole different set of expressions, like the world had turned over and now they were on the other side.

16

That day after the killing, Gentle walked off into the hills. One minute he was on his knees in the square, Indians hollering pitched, the reports of the soldiers' guns coughing through the dusty air. Next thing he knew he was up in the hills overlooking the fort grounds. He still had the knife in his hands. He'd tossed his gun aside, taken the bayonet right off of it. He remembered this from the walk up, but he wasn't sure where he left it. He sat down with the knife. He licked the blade where the dry blood was because he wanted it to be moist again. It seemed important for it to be like that. He carved three lines in his left biceps with the soiled blade. He gritted his teeth in the sun. Then he reached over with his tongue and licked the blood off his arm again. He could reach the place if he bent his neck down. Overhead there were hawks and buzzards. The hawks, high in the air, looked like they were part of the bright red dying sun from where he sat in the dusty dirt. The buzzards were lower. He wished for a minute he had his gun again, for the buzzards. Some of them birds just needed to be shot. That's what they're asking for. Since he was up in the hills, and at least a half a mile from the parade ground, no one could hear him when he started screaming.

They displayed the bodies in the parade grounds. There were three of them. Their wounds, the holes in their bodies looked obscene in the bright sunlight. Any Indian who had been anywhere near the square during the Crazy Horse killing had been placed under heavy guard. Both guardhouses were full. The rest stayed away, up in the hills. All available soldiers had been given orders to march out in the morning and preparations were being made to mount a new campaign to Montana.

The plan, General Crook told his assembled officers at noon in his office, was to head off the Nez Perce somewhere in Montana. We got Gibbon and his fellas on their tail still and we've got three other troops on their way. We're going to pinch them off before they git there.

The officers were filing out, going to check on their commands, when Gentle came in dirty, tired and sweating. He still had the blood on him from when he killed Crazy Horse two days before.

Corporal Ezekial Gentle reporting for duty, sir, he said.

How ya doing, son?

Guess I been better. Guess I'm all right.

You got them holes all done?

They got them done, sir. Just waiting on the word to haul the bodies up to the hills.

Son, we're going to send you back to Gibbon. We're going to send who we can to help with the Nez Perce. Yore boys been in action out in Montana.

Gentle looked at his boots, he started to speak, low at first.

Sir, I just done what I had to. I never knowed nothing, never was nothing 'cept a kid fore I come out here. Gentle raised his head to look full at General Crook. We done started after that Crazy Horse then we just left him there. When I heard he was here, I-I . . .

You just come out here.

I did. That's what I done, sir.

All right then. You done it. That's all. We got to get you out of here, now. You going to be ready to ride out again in the morning?

Guess so. I don't see the point in hanging around.

They piled the bodies in a wagon and hitched up a mule to haul them up the rise to where the holes were. They were hard to handle, and the head of the one Gentle had flopped down weird and hit him in the leg. It didn't hurt or anything but when the long hair fell down and softly fell against his bare arm it felt strange.

They tossed the Indians down in the holes. They picked up their shovels and started throwing the dirt back over them. When they were done, Gentle took out his Bible and read from it.

His new Captain found him later in the stable. He still had the knife and he was carving little lines in a fence post. When Gentle saw the officer, he raised his other hand for a salute.

I hear you know all the country out that way.

I done rode over most of it if that's what ya mean.

You going to be ready to go again in the morning?

That ain't a question you're going to have to ask me, sir.

I guess not.

You ain't heard about what happened out there have ya?

Reports are sketchy. I heard they had some casualties though, Gibbon's troop.

They're still after them then?

That's what we hear.

I got people out there with them.

Is that right. I'm sorry, my name's Morgan.

William Ezekial Gentle.

Morgan had dark red hair and freckles. His beard came out a little lighter. He wasn't much taller than Gentle but he had maybe twenty or thirty pounds on him.

What you doing here?

Trying to count a little I guess.

What's that?

I'm trying to get a feel for how long I been out here. That and maybe how many of them Indians I done killed. I like to see what I'm counting out before me.

Morgan looked at the marks on the fence post. The wood of the post was dark, but the marks Gentle had carved were of lighter color, almost white.

I guess you been out here awhile then.

Guess I have.

They say the Indians are on their last legs. They say that this here Chief Joseph and his all are the last ones.

I don't mind. I ain't got nothing else.

Well, I guess I'll see you in the morning. You got your outfit and all?

I believe I can get a hold of everything I need.

Well, you let me know if you need anything else. You come on real high recommendation from the Gen'l.

Gentle just nodded. He bent down and got some dirt from the ground and rubbed it over the lines he'd carved in his arm.

Dirt's the best thing for it, he said.

Morgan just watched.

This is what I was taught, Gentle went on, this is what I believe. My granny told me that. The blood wants the earth, she used to say, and the earth wants the blood. She said it was in the Bible, but I ain't found the place where yet. I'm going to keep reading though. I don't doubt my granny none.

You do that, Morgan said. He didn't know what else there was to say. When he walked off he felt kind of awkward about it. Later when asked by a buddy about the soldier they called the One Who Killed Crazy Horse, that's what he said.

He has a way of making a man feel unsure.

When his friend asked him what he meant though, he couldn't find the words.

Gentle spent the rest of the night banging out a set of new shoes for his horse. If he was going to be riding again, then he'd have to take care of what was his. When he thought of Bradley, he couldn't picture his face in his mind and it troubled him. He could see Huebner easy enough. He could hear how low his voice was. He wondered why it was like that. He could think of all of Bradley's features, the color of his eyes, the way he stood in the sun, with the horses by a creek after a long hard day in the saddle. He could see his hat, pulled back to wipe the sweat off his forehead. He could even picture his hand, the way he waved when he was far off and he wanted the others to ride up and talk about something. But he couldn't see his face. He didn't like to think of it much. He preferred not to think about anything much at all. When his horse whinnied a bit, he petted its flank. He brushed him down for over an hour that night.

When Gentle walked out in the square, he could see the blood still there, on the dirt in the moonlight, from where the Indian had fallen at his hands. He walked over and rubbed out the spot with his boot. There were some men singing the old songs under one of the trees. Gentle could tell from the sound of their voices that they were drunk. The moonlight lit up the grounds and turned the dirt almost white. Back in Tennessee where he came from, up in the mountains the dirt was black. It'd been a long time since he'd seen it. After a while the General came up and they got to talking.

Well, I done rode here. I guess. I can ride back.

That's what you done, son.

Wish I felt better about what I was.

We all wish for something, son.

They went over to the fire then, and joined the others. Gentle took what was offered to him from the bottle.

I never seem to sleep too well the night before I go out, Gentle said.

It's not that kind of time, someone else said.

When it started raining an hour or so before dawn, they sat there, under the old tree. The drops that came in through the branches were warm and they felt good. The soldiers got quiet then, all of them drinking, sitting under the leaves and watching the rain.

When Huebner saw the campfires blazing on the mountains overhead, and then the bluecoats gathered round in the deepening twilight, he wondered if it meant he would live or he would die. Either way he felt a lifting of his heart. He had walked the last four days. He felt awful about what they'd done to Baker, but there was nothing he could do about that. Maybe it was different for the Indians, to just leave someone like that. It was maybe a week before when he'd gotten sick. First it was a cough and then the phlegm turned from blue to blood. When the poor boy started raving and his legs didn't work anymore, Huebner tried to drag him, arms over his shoulders helping him walk. He thought if they knew they might shoot him right there. In the end a couple of the braves came over. When the boy fell down, they pulled Huebner off him.

What do you think they're going to do us?

Baker's question hurt Huebner's heart.

They could drop us off or kill us, either one. Maybe what they want to do is trade us, he told him.

I hope they get a good deal.

For a couple a broke down soldiers, I don't know.

Everything's got its price, brother, Baker said. The wheezing sound he made so faint like wind through the grass.

You think.

Got to, Baker said, and coughed. It's all right, he said, and blinked. Just let me lie here awhile.

Huebner swallowed, wiped the dust from his eyes.

G'wan, Baker said, leave me here to rest awhile.

When Huebner embraced him, he could feel his chest pant. When Huebner started crying, he had to turn away.

It was early in the morning with the dew still on the grass. They'd been up all night together. He wished he'd known some Bible verses so he could have said them over with him. In the end all he could do was listen, wipe the sweat off his brow, not turn away from his breath turned so foul. He didn't even know the Our Father prayer. He always just mouthed the words with Gentle and Bradley. When they tied him up on the horse and pulled it away, he looked back for a long time. There was a clutch of cottonwood trees, blown bare by the relentless wind, way out in the middle of a wide open field, where they left Baker.

From then on he was alone. They took him down off the horse. He didn't run; he didn't cry. He tried not even to blink his eyes, as he felt them tear from the wind when it came up fierce all day, blowing so much of the gray white dirt on him that when they stopped to lie down that night his pants were almost white. He knew a few of the Indians now, by the way they moved, the ones that were with him. They didn't treat him badly or well. He was just there with them and he stopped wondering why.

He saw the troopers' horses first. When he realized it was the saddles that made them funny, he knew he wasn't alone anymore. They were ahead in the path the Indians had taken. That night they built a great fire themselves and tied him right up in front of it. They danced and they sang. They cut off pieces of his hair and they all touched him, all of the warriors. They pricked each of his fingers one at the time and mixed his blood with the paint they put on their faces.

It don't hurt any.

Huebner spoke out loud to them. It was a way not to give in.

Those are the stars up there, he said. It was just this voice that came out of him. It didn't make any sense and he didn't think about it. He imagined he was talking to his son. He knew he didn't have one, but it didn't matter. Maybe someday he would. He would remember all this and it would be over.

They come out at night and light the way all the way up to heaven, he said.

As the night wore on he saw other fires, the blinking of the flames in the distance, the gray smoke carrying off against the half-moon lit sky. That must have been when he first fell asleep. He woke to a terrible smell. A warrior held a burning stick to his bare chest. When another brave with a fat belly and legs as thick as stumps burned both his arms, he didn't even feel it. He watched the sparks dance off the last flames. He heard their songs and their chirping voices like he heard the crickets, just sounds that filled up the night.

Gentle rode through the night and slept a couple hours in the heat of the day. He rode way up ahead of the troopers. He liked what it looked like in the night to turn back of a rise and see them, off in the distance, by the dust that rose off all the horses, gray, blown in the night air, or by the smoke off their fires when they'd stopped for the night. The sky was an inverted bowl of stars over the long rolling hills. When he slit his eyes close it looked like the earth had skin and it was bunched up in places. Each night as it got late and the dark turned to a vision, he could see the great lights shimmering to the north. They lit his way and told him where the Indians were heading. It looked so pretty he didn't blame them at all. It was like the heat that he saw rising off the ground in streams during the day was still there in the dark, was drawn up toward the stars by some power he didn't understand. The lights twinkled and reached into the sky like a carpet to the heavens. For hours he would just let the horse take him drifting in and out of sleep, listening to the sound the hooves made when they hit on the hard-packed earth of the desert plains. He liked to be alone. He rode harder whenever he felt lonesome. It sure was big out there. It did funny things to a man's mind. A couple times he stopped and just lay down to wait for the other soldiers to catch up. It wouldn't do any good to get too far ahead. Or he rode with the Arikawas. He liked them because they were there but they would never talk to him. They'd picked up the trail a week or so back and were now following through the high desert plains right behind the Indians. They found a lone soldier left dead.

What the hell? someone said.

Goddamn, said another.

He had crawled a long, long way and then he died out there in the middle of a long field. He'd been stripped bare and the ones that found him had to chase some dogs away from what was left. The only thing was a bullet that came out of his hand when he lost hold of it and died. Gentle and some of the Indians buried him right out there in the middle of the field. One of the soldiers picked up the bullet but Gentle made him leave it there.

It's all we got to mark the spot.

He didn't want to make the fool feel bad. But he couldn't believe he wanted to take away from one of their own dead. It was all the poor boy had. They buried the man and rode on. They rode the trail a few more days before they caught up with the Indians. Morgan went ahead with his Sergeants to report to command. Gentle found Gibbon's troop camped on a bare dirt rise. The wind had come on cold and full of mist as the sun went down behind the mountains. All that was left were a few greenhorns, scared to death. There wasn't even anyone to talk to and ask about Huebner and Bradley.

Oh y'mean that Captain. That was a man that looked good on his horse.

Where is he damnit? Is he alive or dead?

Ahh now, we're the only ones. We all got broke apart. Maybe he was with those we lost way on back there, way on back there.

Gentle couldn't even yell at them. It was all so pitiful. They could hardly talk a sentence.

They begged for food and tobacco. They all looked sort of dazed. There was one old man who said his name was Black.

They're all gone, 'cept us and the Colonel. We followed these Ned Percys for weeks now. Joined up with Howard's boys back at Canyon Creek.

When was that?

Couple weeks ago, I giss. All run together now. We got up to them here. We had a battle. A stand-off. Then y'all's troop come on.

Gentle didn't know what to say, he didn't have to believe them so he decided that he wouldn't. He spit on the ground and walked away.

They were in the highlands, long rolling grassy fields, with ice in the streams in the morning, dew frozen on the grass. They laid their bedrolls in the open, overlooking what was left of the Indian camp. They had retreated into a deep glen of red weeds that sheltered a long creek cut.

You find your old troop yet? Morgan asked him. They stood by a fire, waiting for orders, sharing a smoke.

I heard some things. Gentle spat, picked a leaf from his tongue. They're all messed up, they're liable to say anything, he said to Captain Morgan.

That's right. We'll find your boys out here yet.

Gentle scuffed his boot in the dirt. He didn't have to get sentimental about it. He wasn't a kid.

General Miles done met with their Chief once, Morgan said. He's about ready to give in. I guess we'll go in hard tomorrow to make sure. These Ned Percys is one stubborn bunch of red men.

He called his command over to his fire. He didn't drink though he didn't mind at all if the others did. Gentle joined him over a tin cup of coffee, which he spiked just a little with some whiskey from one of the other officers.

Gentle spent the rest of the night with the Arikawas. They called out to the wolves all night. He liked what it sounded like when they answered back. He watched the fires of the Nez Perce down below. He'd kept the wound on his right arm open since they'd left Nebraska Territory. It was something about the way the pain made him feel. He liked it and he thought it helped his gun. He drew blood from his arm and rubbed it on the barrel and cleaned it by moonlight to pass the time until dawn.

At the river crossing where the troops all came together, it was cool in the shade under the immense clouds, at the northernmost fork of the Musselshell River, beautiful and lush green grass meadow, marshy lakes with ducks. The men slept under the stars on a river plateau. Down a long stepped draw the Nez Perce had taken cover in a tall grass ravine. In the morning it rained hard. With the sounding of the thunder, the first Gatling gun started sputtering out bullets toward the teepees of the Indian encampment. The first spurts of bullets kicked up the dirt by the creek cut and turned the water brown with mud. As the gunner, a kid named Levie Britt from Georgia, pulled the gun, the bullets started to slice through the water. They made a hissing sound as they went down below the surface and stuck in the mud. His partner Stimmons, a volunteer from Texarkana, stuck another rock under the gun. He did this while Britt was still cranking the bullets out, and lost control of the gun. The barrel turned once all the way around, sending bullets into the dirt wall of the butte behind them, into the creek below and far off into the first teepee line of the Indian village.

Huebner was still tied to the post. The sky was cracked with sunshine and what looked like a nice cloudless day far off in the distance. Overhead the clouds hung gray. He was soaked. Thunder sounded, and lightning singed the sky with electric light. A brave came walking toward him. His face ran blue in the rain. When he reached Huebner, he pulled a knife from his boot moccasin and slit all the ropes. Huebner crumpled to the ground and he just left him there in the mud. The Indian gave an ear-piercing scream and ran off through the gathering puddles to join the others.

The guns were set up in three places: on a bluff overlooking the water, in the distance where there was a chasm cut between two buttes and in the middle of the two, up a sheer rock-face.

What was left of Gibbon's troop had been dispatched as cannon fodder for the village and a few of them got hit too. This gave the Nez Perce time to get out their guns. They set up a sniper line on their stomachs by the water, and started picking off the soldiers coming down the hill. The women and children were taken out the back way. They just ran into the open across the long field. Huebner saw them go. He was lying there beside the charred and smoking ruins of last night's fire. He heard the soft pats of the running feet on the mud, the sharp commanding cries of the mothers after their children. He saw one little child fall from her mother's arms and bounce along the ground. Then he passed out again.

Morgan led his men down the hill after the fleeing Indians. Gentle ran out ahead and took the lead. They met no resistance at all from the women and children.

Stop it! Stop it now, he called out. They don't even have no guns.

A couple of Pawnee mercenaries had already started taking scalps. Gentle raised his gun and shot them both in the chest. Then he walked over and shot dead the blood-crowned Indians writhing on the ground, feeling with their hands in spasms for the bloody places that were the tops of their heads.

Let's just round em up, Morgan said when he could speak again. He threw up on the run coming up behind Gentle, when he saw what he had done, got it all over his pants.

When Britt on the hill finally got the gun right he aimed for the creek where the last of Gibbon's survivors were now splashing through the water dark red and brown. The bullets knocked down soldiers and Indians alike when they did hit something, and crashed in the water when they didn't. Britt was crying now and couldn't move his fingers as he steered the gun in a line back and forth over the water. He kept shooting long after there was nothing else standing.

He didn't even see the Indians. They'd climbed up the bluff and came in from the rear. A tomahawk split his head wide open and he just sat down again with his hand on the gun. Stimmons smelled his partner's flesh, he saw Britt had fallen and ran off. The gun kept turning of its own momentum and it gave Stimmons time to dive headfirst down the bluff. He rolled with his hands over his face, down through the dirt and tall grass clumps, splashing into the water himself with the rest of the bodies down there.

Under a drizzle, Morgan and Gentle put guns in the back of the prisoners, women with bare backs and breasts tanned and exposed to the sun, with their babes slung over their shoulders in rawhide papooses. An old man who kept dropping to his knees, and calling out in a holler toward the sky, with the rain wetting his upturned face. Gentle took a kid by one hand, a little girl with long hair that almost covered her bare ass. She was crying and Gentle felt bad for her. They had a long line of captives that they herded into a milling pack. They walked from the middle of the field toward the chasm at the foot of the two great buttes.

The Nez Perce had taken the gun from Lee and Stimmons. They turned the crank and aimed it, but all of the bullets fell short now. They finally just pushed the whole thing down the hill and watched it kick up dirt and then tumble down into the creek with a crash. They tied white cloths around their heads and went off to follow the long line of Indians retreating toward the two bluffs.

By noon, General Miles had taken charge of the Nez Perce camp and sent the other Commander's man Hoey to round up any stragglers. They were the ones that found Huebner. They thought he was just another dead Indian at first, even though he had a blue coat on. His pants were just ripped streamer rags. His skin was brown from the sun and the dirt and the dried blood. One of the men kicked him over, saw him open his mouth then his eyes. No words come out.

Give that man a water drink, someone said. He's one of our'n and he ain't dead.

Gentle spread all the men out in a long circle around the captive Indians. Miles walked out toward the middle of the field with a long line of troopers to meet the warriors tromping through the field. He saw the white on their heads. He watched them toss down their guns. They did it one at a time. Each of them hollered and went down to his knees in the rain. They rose and met the soldiers there in the field.

Just round em up, men, just round them up, General Miles said.

The rain moved on around four o'clock, half of the field full of Indians were in the sun and half of them still pelted with rain. When night finally fell, the sky was clear and the moon came out.

General Miles led the group of warriors into the pack through the chain of soldiers around them. Gentle found Huebner then. The troopers had come back with him. His new Captain, Morgan, pulled Gentle aside, said, There's something you should see.

They had pulled the Colonel Gibbon out to look at Huebner. Gibbon had come into the camp with the last of his survivors but had finally run out of alcohol. All during the attack he could be seen biting his uniform sleeves and calling out after things no one else saw. He shook uncontrollably, broke into sweats and shivered in the warm rain. For a moment when he saw Huebner everything was clear: he just starting crying and they left him there. It was an awful thing for anyone else to look at.

Man used to be a Colonel, someone said.

Ain't even a dog now.

Gibbon fell down to where Huebner lay and wrapped his arms around the man. That's when Gentle walked up. He just shook his head. He took off his hat and kneeled down with the two men in the mud.

C'mon now, Colonel, Gentle said. He patted the crying man on the shoulder. C'mon now, it's all right.

Gentle pried Gibbon's arms out from around the fallen soldier. He got out his own canteen, poured some water in his hand and started to rub the water into Huebner's face. Gentle sat with him there, long after the Colonel went away.

They left the dead on the field, Indians and troopers both, in the creek, lying in the murky water with the gun that killed them all, with the teepees still standing, like little ship sails in the sea of darkness out there in the field. As the stars came twinkling on, the soldiers set out with the Indians walking in a long ragged line and mounted soldiers in a moving chain around them. They herded them all together to a long meadow over the first rise and made camp for the night.

Gentle got someone to help him lift Huebner into one of the Gatling buckboards, empty now with the gun lost. Gentle kept one hand on his rifle, the other on Huebner's shoulder and watched the sky. The moon was full and lit up the faces of the Indians, sharing what few blankets they had, huddled together for the cold. When Gentle looked in one's eyes Gentle was the first to turn away. At some point Huebner started talking. It was all just a big mess. It seemed like Huebner had something to tell him. He would pull at Gentle's pants legs when he looked away. It was hard to look at Huebner because when he talked his lips moved funny and drool came out of his mouth and wet down his neck. He talked about his forehead and bone, birds in the sky, crickets, grasshoppers and skeeters. He talked about an Indian shot, shot, shot, shot. He said it just like that. Said he was dancing backwards and he talked about his pocket. When Gentle reached in there that's when he found the piece of tin. He could see it good enough in the moonlight to tell what it was. When the sun started to rise, purple first, then soft and yellow in the distance over the long, rolling plain behind them, they were still there, the troopers with their guns raised on their knees, nodding off on their watch. Gentle sat in the wagon holding one hand on Huebner's shoulder and the other now clutched around the small piece of tin with the Lieutenant's name punched in it.

It's all right, Gentle whispered. He wished he could have done something, or at least been there when Bradley fell. He wanted to say more, but he didn't. Huebner was too far gone and there was no one else.

This is a work of fiction. All of the main characters in this book were real people. Some will be recognized as historical figures and others are lost to time. All of the battles are real, as is the time scheme: June 1876 to September 1877. August Huebner was my great-great-grandfather. Family myth says that he went to fight with Custer but arrived a day late. This is the story that called to me. James Bradley is known as the first soldier to discover the Custer massacre, William Gentle as the killer of Crazy Horse.

ACKNOWLEDGMENTS

The author would like to thank Simon Green; Geoff Kloske; Dan Green; David Rosenthal; Nicole Graev; Julie H. Forbes; Sarah Manges; Abby Thomas; Catherine Luttinger; Bret Ellis; Tony Williams; Maggie Estep; Ingalill Wahlroos; Jim Coleman; Louise Wareham; William Georgiades; Frank Britt; Barry Alexander Brown; Jennifer Busch; Brian Keener; Regina Robin; Stephen Wright; Wendy Rasmussen; Sara Crosby; Jackson Taylor; Lousie DeSalvo; Sarah Graham Hayes; Howie Sanders; Richard Green; David Winn; Grant Bull-Tail, storyteller of the Crow Indian tribe; and in memoriam, Clayton Brooks Williamson.